RUNAWAY

Also by Wendelin Van Draanen

How I Survived Being a Girl
Flipped
Swear to Howdy
Confessions of a Serial Kisser
The Running Dream
The Secret Life of Lincoln Jones

The Sammy Keyes Mysteries

Sammy Keyes and the Hotel Thief
Sammy Keyes and the Skeleton Man
Sammy Keyes and the Sisters of Mercy
Sammy Keyes and the Runaway Elf
Sammy Keyes and the Curse of Moustache Mary
Sammy Keyes and the Hollywood Mummy
Sammy Keyes and the Search for Snake Eyes
Sammy Keyes and the Art of Deception
Sammy Keyes and the Psycho Kitty Queen
Sammy Keyes and the Dead Giveaway
Sammy Keyes and the Wild Things
Sammy Keyes and the Cold Hard Cash
Sammy Keyes and the Wedding Crasher
Sammy Keyes and the Night of Skulls
Sammy Keyes and the Power of Justice Jack
Sammy Keyes and the Showdown in Sin City
Sammy Keyes and the Killer Cruise
Sammy Keyes and the Kiss Goodbye

Wendelin Van Draanen

RUNAWAY

EMBER

All rights reserved. Published in the United States by Ember, an imprint of Random House Children's Books, a division of Penguin Random House LLC, New York. Originally published in hardcover in the United States by Alfred A. Knopf, an imprint of Random House Children's Books, New York, in 2006.

Ember and the E colophon are registered trademarks of Penguin Random House LLC.

Visit us on the Web! randomhouseteens.com

Educators and librarians, for a variety of teaching tools, visit us at RHTeachersLibrarians.com

The Library of Congress has cataloged the hardcover edition of this work as follows:
Van Draanen, Wendelin.
Runaway / Wendelin Van Draanen. — 1st ed.
p. cm.
Summary: After running away from her fifth foster home, Holly, a twelve-year-old orphan, travels across the country, keeping a journal of her experiences and struggle to survive.
ISBN 978-0-375-83522-3 (trade) — ISBN 978-0-375-93522-0 (lib. bdg.) —
ISBN 978-0-375-84912-1 (ebook)
[1. Runaways—Fiction. 2. Homeless persons—Fiction. 3. Orphans—Fiction.
4. Survival—Fiction. 5. Diaries—Fiction.] I. Title.
PZ7.V2857Ru 2006
[Fic]—dc22
2005033276

ISBN 978-0-307-97597-3 (tr. pbk.)

Printed in the United States of America
10
First Ember Edition 2012

Random House Children's Books supports the First Amendment and celebrates the right to read.

RUNAWAY

May 17th

It's cold. It's late. I'm trapped in here, trying to sleep under this sorry excuse for a blanket, and I've just got to tell you—you don't know squat. You *think* you know what I'm going through, you *think* you know how I can "cope," but you're just like everybody else: clueless. Writing. Poetry. Learning to express myself. "It'll help you turn the page, Holly. Just try it."

Well, I'm trying it, see? And is it making me feel better? NO! Giving me this journal was a totally *lame* thing to do. You think writing will get me out of here? You think *words* will make me forget about the past? Get real, Ms. Leone!

Words can't fix my life.

Words can't give me a family.

I

Words can't do jack.

You may be a teacher, Ms. Leone, but face it: You don't know squat.

May 19th

Oh, you really took the cake today. "Put your most embarrassing experience in the form of a cinquain poem." What did you expect me to do? Write the truth? I knew you'd read them out loud, and you did! How do *you* spell *idiot*? I spell it L-E-O-N-E.

Did you like my little poem about spilling my milk in a restaurant? Stupid, I know, so give me an F, see if I care. Like I can even remember ever *being* in a real restaurant.

You want a cinquain poem about a most embarrassing moment that actually happened to me? Okay, here you go:

Prisoner
Chained outside
Shivering, huddling, sobbing
Naked in the rain
Alone

Oh, yeah. That makes me feel SO much better.

May 20th

My mom died two years ago today.

I'd been scamming food, she'd been shooting up.

I miss her.

More than I have tears to cry, I miss her.

May 20th, again

You want to know why I was crying at recess? That cat Camille is why. She called me a homeless freak. Told me I had a face only my mother could love. Normally, I would have told her to eat dirt and die, but today I just couldn't take it.

I didn't tell you because I knew you wouldn't believe me. Everyone knows she's your favorite. "Miss Leone, do you need some help?" "Miss Leone, do you want *me* to pass those out?" "Oh, Miss Leone, you look so pretty today!" Adopt her, why don't you?

Oh, that's right—she already *has* two parents.

May 20th again, again

When they moved me in with the Benders, the social worker told me that they were "very kind and very patient people." What a laugh. They're phonies, is what they are. Mrs. Bender is a heartless witch, and Mr. Bender is a total creep. He's always touching me. On the shoulder. On the hair. On the hand. He gets that same look that Mr. Fisk used to get when *his* wife wasn't around.

Social services won't believe me if I complain. They'll say I'm just looking for trouble. Lying. Faking. Overreacting. "Self-inflicting."

Well, I'm not going through that again. I'd rather DIE than go through that again. So tonight when Mr. Bender started massaging my shoulders, I told him, "Stop it!"

He didn't. "I'm only trying to help you unwind," he said in his snaky voice.

"Stop it!" I shouted. "Don't touch me!" And I slapped his creepy hands away.

That brought Mrs. Bender running. "What is going on in here?" she asked, and after *he* explained it to her, I got locked in my room. Not the room they show the social worker. That's the room they tell me I'll get when I'm a "good" girl. The room I *really* get is the laundry room. They give me a mat, a blanket, and a bucket to pee in.

So sweet dreams, Ms. Leone, in your feathery bed or whatever you have.

Do you really believe *words* are going to keep me warm and safe tonight?

May 21st, early morning

Why am I doing this? Why am I writing to you again? I'm shivering in this room, huddled under this blanket writing to you, and why? What good is it? I'm hungry, I can't sleep, I'm locked in here, and I've got to pee. I hate using the bucket, I just hate it.

Man, I've got to go. Hold on a minute.

Oh, that's better.

Maybe I can get back to sleep now.

Nope. I'm too cold.

So you want to hear how I get a drink when they trap me in here on weekends? I turn on the washer. Pretty sly, huh? I used to put my

4

blanket in the dryer and get it roasting hot, but the dryer quit working and of course I got blamed.

I don't mind the size of this squatty little room, it's the cold that gets me. Why can't they give me a better blanket? How about a sleeping bag? Would that kill them?

Whatever. No matter how much I try, I'll never be "good" enough to sleep in the real room.

I've got to come up with a plan to get *out* of here.

May 21st again, lunchtime

What is it with you and poetry? It's like some crazy obsession with you. And I couldn't believe your stupid "Life is poetry" statement. Maybe *your* life is poetry, but mine's a pile of four-letter words. "Find the motion. Find the rhythm. Find the *timbre* of your life." Whose idea *is* all this? Yours? Did somebody teach you this stuff? How's this ever going to help me in life?

And guess what? You can forget it. I'm not doing it. Write your own stupid poem about your own poetic life.

Mine would just get me sent to the office.

May 21st again again, after school

I hate you, you know that? I hate you for making me write that poem. I hate you for making me lie about my life. But most of all I hate you for acting so sweet to me. You don't *really* care. I'm a job to you, like I am to everybody else. I know it, so quit pretending you care.

And you probably think you're doing a *good* job, but guess what? You're not. I can see right through you, so just leave me alone, would

5

you? Forget I'm even in your class. Forget you're supposed to be trying to "help" me. And quit making me write poems!

May 21st again again AGAIN, after school

How stupid are all these *agains*, huh? I'm not doing that anymore. Four entries in one day is ridiculous, anyway. But before I turn the corner and go into the Benders' house, I just had to tell you that there *is* something good in my life.

Dogs.

I love dogs. They're so happy and loyal and soft. The Benders don't have one, are you kidding? Wouldn't want to mess up their perfect house. But on my walk home from school I usually get to say hello to a few, and there's this one black Labrador I call Blackie that I get to see every day.

Blackie's old and pretty lame and sleeps on the side of the street where the asphalt can warm his bones. First time I saw him, I thought he was a dead homeless dog because he looked like some of the dead homeless *people* I've seen. But after I checked him out, I discovered he was fine, just really old. I brought him scraps from the cafeteria the next day, and ever since, he waits for me on the corner. He's a sweet old guy, and I sit and talk to him a lot. He's a real good listener, and I think he'd follow me home if he could.

Me and him cuddled up on the laundry-room floor.

Sounds like heaven.

May 21st, evening

This journal's nothing but trouble, you hear me? I ought to just throw it away and be done with it.

How can a journal be trouble, you ask?

Here's how:

For two months I've been walking home to the Benders' instead of taking the bus. I figured out in a hurry that there was no sense in rushing home. So for two months I've been enjoying that little half hour of freedom when I'm not in school having to listen to Camille kiss up to you, and not at the Benders' getting blamed for something. I walk through the park, visit with Blackie . . . it's the best part of my day.

But today I went and made the mistake of sitting on the curb and writing in this stupid journal. I just *had* to tell you about Blackie.

What a moron I am. It's not like you actually heard.

It's not like you'd even *care.*

But I had to go and stop and sit and write, and what did it get me?

All upset, for one thing. I don't *like* to talk about stuff like wanting a dog. What's the use in it? It's never going to happen, so why waste time dreaming about it?

But on top of getting me upset, it also made me late, and late to the Benders' meant that I was buying drugs.

"I wasn't buying drugs!" I told them. "I was petting a dog!"

They tore apart my backpack, shouting, "Don't lie to us, girl! Where have you been? Why weren't you riding the bus? How long have you been lying to us?"

I skipped the riding-the-bus question. Like they'd believe me anyway?

But I told them fifty times that I didn't do drugs, didn't buy drugs or sell drugs or want anything to *do* with drugs, but when they didn't find any drugs in my backpack, they still made me strip down to my underwear.

And when Mrs. Bender had gone through every nook and cranny of those, you know what she muttered when she shoved my clothes back at me?

"Well, your mama sure did."

I almost hit her. But I started crying instead.

I *hate* that.

I hate *her.*

And here I am in laundry-room lockdown again.

For being a "bad girl."

Excuse me for walking home.

Excuse me for petting a dog.

Excuse me for wanting to breathe some *air.*

So see? If I get in trouble for *that,* what would've happened to me if they'd bothered to look inside *this*? They don't care beans about my schoolwork. Everyone knows I'm a "behavioral problem," so it's not their fault that I'm flunking sixth grade, right? They're the saints who've taken me in when nobody else wanted me.

But if they had even bothered to flip through this book, they would have read what I wrote about them, and then look out! I would have been in way worse trouble than lockdown with no supper.

Bottom line, this journal's not only stupid, it's dangerous.

Tomorrow, first chance I get, I'm burning it.

May 22nd, morning

Before I burn this, I have to tell you one more thing. You'll faint when you hear.

Ready?

I dreamt a *poem* last night.

Hey (slap-slap-slap), wake up! You should have been sitting down (ha ha).

You want to hear?

Okay. Here goes:

> There once was a doggie named Blackie
> Who couldn't exactly attacky
> But he drooled and he licked
> Drowned the Benders real quick
> Floated off and they never came backy!

Funny, huh? It's a limerick! (Yeah, yeah, you already knew that, I know.)

Okay. That's it. Now I'm torching this.

I just need to score a match.

May 22nd, midmorning

Crud. I'm going to have to wait for Monday to burn this because it looks like I'm not getting out of the house until then.

Why?

Because I got busted looking for a match.

9

"What are you stealing now, girl?" Mrs. Bender asked when she saw me looking through a kitchen cupboard. Then she yanked me back by my hair until I was looking up at the ceiling.

I hate when she does that. It makes me want to cut my hair short. But I did that when I ran away from the Fisks and my neck was cold the whole time.

Big deal, huh? It's just your neck, right?

Wrong. When your neck's cold, so's the rest of you. Try sleeping outside sometime with everything covered but your neck. It makes your whole body shivering cold.

So I've got hair that covers my neck, but the trade-off is that now I've got to put up with people like Mrs. Bender grabbing it and steering me around.

And while she had me looking at the ceiling, you know what saintly Mrs. Bender did?

She called, "How-ie!" across the house at Mr. Bender. "This girl's ransacking our cupboards!"

"I wasn't ransacking!" I croaked. "I was just looking for a toothpick!"

What's the harm in taking a toothpick, right? But she pulled harder on the fistful of hair and said, "And you think stealing our toothpicks is okay?"

"I wasn't stealing them!" I gasped. "I just need *one*. Or some floss. Can I have some floss? I have food stuck between my teeth."

It was a pretty good lie, don't you think? And I sounded pretty convincing, too. But she just shouted, "How-ie! I told you! This girl's a thief!"

So see? I use drugs and I'm a thief.

Then Mr. Bender came into the kitchen, saying, "I just checked my wallet—there's fifty dollars missing!"

They searched my stuff again.

Stripped me down again.

Called me a thief and a liar and a bad girl again.

Which is why I'm in lockdown for the rest of the weekend.

Again.

May 22nd, afternoon

I've been thinking: The way Mrs. Bender went through my stuff looking for the missing money wasn't very thorough. Nothing like when she was searching for drugs.

You know what else?

Mrs. Bender *loves* the shopping network. I swear she spends the whole day watching jewelry twinkle on TV.

So you know what I think?

I think she wants stuff that her creepy husband won't let her get. I think she wants to peg me as a thief because *she's* been stealing money out of his wallet.

Money social services gives him for taking care of *me*.

May 22nd, nighttime

What are you supposed to do in a laundry room all day? They did let me out for ten minutes when I pounded on the door and shouted that I really had to use the bathroom, but I got locked right back in. And around six Mrs. Bender shoved a plate of cold mashed-potato mush at me and said, "You need to think long and hard about your actions, girl, because actions have consequences." That was it for the entire day.

So you know what I did? I read that stupid book you gave us. "Don't read ahead, class. Do NOT read ahead! We want to stay together and discuss it as a group. If you want to do extra reading, read from another book."

Well, guess what? I don't happen to have another book. There's no library tucked away inside this luxurious laundry room. All I happen to have is my binder, this stupid journal, and your little discussion book.

So sue me. I read ahead. Clear to the end.

And I knew it. I just knew it. The girl dies. Why do teachers think books where people die are such good books? They're rotten, you hear me? Who wants to read about people drowning or getting cancer or finding out their parents are dead? Or you know what's even worse? *Dogs* dying. If a teacher's having you read a book with a dog in it, the dog's going to be dead by the end of the book. I hate that! Why do they always have to kill off the dog?

Maybe you teachers think books like that open our eyes and prepare us for life, but guess what? All they do is teach us that life is cruel and people are mean and there's not squat we can do to change it.

Like this is something I didn't already know?

Sunday, May 23rd

Sundays terrify me. Every Sunday morning at 9:30 Mrs. Bender leaves the house to pick up her mother and take her to church. After church they go shopping and out to lunch, which means I'm home alone with Mr. Bender from 9:30 until about 2:00.

"Are you going to be a good girl today?" he always asks through the laundry-room door when she's gone.

I used to argue that I *had* been good and that I hadn't meant to make them mad, or whatever. But it didn't take long to get the picture that there was no way I was going to win that argument, so I'd just grumble, "Yes, sir," and he'd let me out and fix pancakes and bacon and eggs, chatting about nothing the whole time.

It's not like the Benders starve me, but if it wasn't for my school lunch card and Sunday morning breakfasts, I'd have, like, zero hot meals a week.

Not that hot lunch is actually *hot,* but it's a whole lot better than the slop Mrs. Bender shoves at me through the laundry-room door.

So Sunday mornings are torture for me. I love the smell of bacon. I love pancakes and syrup and butter. My mouth's watering just thinking about them.

But Mr. Bender is so creepy, and being alone in the house with him makes me real skittish. He always says, "Relax, Holly. We'll just have us a nice breakfast and get to know each other a little better." Then he gives me a snaky wink as he cracks open an egg and says, "It'll be our little secret, all right?"

So I've started thinking that the breakfast isn't worth the price of admission. I don't like putting up with his snaky ways for the rest of the day. He brushes up against me. Touches my shoulder while I'm doing the dishes. Says "soothing" things to me that tie me up in knots.

I'm always relieved when his witchy wife pulls up and he tells me it's time to get back in the laundry room.

You think I'm overreacting, don't you? Inventing. You think maybe Mr. Bender is just being fatherly and I'm ultrasensitive because of Mr. Fisk? Well, guess again. Today when Mrs. Bender left and he said, "Are you going to be a good girl today?" I decided, Forget it. "No, Mr. Bender, I'm not," I told him. "I'm a liar and a thief and I do drugs, so you'd better not let me out of here."

He opened the door anyway. Then he laughed and said, "Come on, Holly, let's have us some breakfast."

"No," I told him. "I'm sick of you accusing me of stuff all week and then acting like nothing's wrong when your wife's gone." I stepped out of the laundry room and headed down the hall. "But I *will* use the bathroom."

So I locked myself in the bathroom, which wasn't much better than being in the laundry room.

Except that I could flush, of course.

But after a minute he knocked and said, "Are we having breakfast?"

"No!" I shouted through the door. "Just leave me alone!"

Next thing I knew, he had the lock popped and was *inside* the bathroom. I was on the toilet and he just barged in!

"Get out, you pervert!" I screamed at him, but he just stood there. So I grabbed this can of Lysol spray that was right next to the toilet and *vooooosh*, I sprayed it in his eyes while I called him every awful name I could think of.

He yowled, then smacked me across the head so hard I fell off the toilet. Then he grabbed me by my hair, slammed up the toilet seat, shoved my head in the bowl, and flushed.

"Don't you *ever* use language like that in my house!"

"You're sick!" I screamed at him when he let me up for air. Regular contaminated toilet water would have been bad enough, but the Benders use that disgusting blue Sani-Flush stuff in their toilets, and my eyes were stinging from the chemicals. I yanked up my pants and called him all sorts of names *again* because I was mortified and totally grossed out.

So he grabbed me by the hair *again,* shoved my face in the toilet and flushed *again,* and this time I thought I was going to drown.

He shouted, "You have a lot to learn about your place in this world, girl! This is *my* house and you'll do as *I* say or there'll be consequences!"

My heart was beating so fast, my arms were flailing around, I couldn't hold my breath much longer. And as blue water seeped into my ears, I heard him say, "You need to learn who's boss around here."

When he finally let me up, I coughed and sputtered, and he could tell what I was thinking, because he threw a towel at me and said, "No one'll believe you. Now get back in your room, girl."

I knew he was right. They hadn't believed me about Mr. Fisk, either, and there had been a lot more proof than a Sani-Flushed head. So I took the towel and staggered back to the laundry room, where I just lay down on my mat and cried.

I hate crying. I hate even saying that I did it, and I sure don't want people *seeing* me do it. And I wouldn't even tell you that part except that the crying made me mad, and getting mad is what made me get off my duff and wash my hair.

How did I wash my hair?

Well, I'm not stupid, you know.

Okay, maybe you don't know, considering my grades, but I don't care about those. I care about getting disgusting blue chemicals off me.

What I did was, I turned the washer on HOT, stuck my head in, and rinsed my hair as well as I could. Then I took the liquid-laundry-soap cap, filled it up with water, swished it around until it dissolved the little bit of soap inside it, and washed my hair with that.

I'm really glad I didn't go for the direct soap. Laundry soap is *strong*. Even the little bit I used sudsed my hair up like crazy. Then I rinsed again and used the cap for reaching the parts I couldn't get by sticking my head in the washer.

I also washed my face and rinsed my mouth out real well.

That blue stuff is *vile*.

Hey, you should try it sometime, just for the experience. Just to see how poetic my life really is.

Oh, wait. How about this for the rhythm and feel of my poetic life:

Blue face
Disgusting taste
Flush it
Shush it
Cold disgrace

I don't think it fits into any of the categories on your handy-dandy poetry sheet, but I don't seem to fit in anywhere, either, so what the heck.

Where was I? Oh, yeah. So I got all cleaned up, and I started making a mental list of what I need to survive on my own. And you know what I've decided?

I only need one thing: a Hefty sack.

Last time I ran away I brought stuff like food and *toilet* paper.

Like you can't survive without toilet paper?

I was dumb. Food you can steal. Toilet paper you can go into any fast-food place and *use.* That kind of stuff is disposable, and you don't need to lug it around and have it slow you down.

What you can't really survive without is warmth, and the biggest enemy of warmth is wet. You get wet, you get cold. Easy as *brrrrrrrr.*

So to keep from getting cold, you need something waterproof. Even when it's not raining, the air gets damp at night, so you get wet, you get cold.

Camille, I'm sure, has a whole wardrobe of ponchos, raincoats, umbrellas, and rain boots to choose from, but me, I've got nothing but a pathetic umbrella that turns inside out in the wind.

I'm not looking to score a whole wardrobe like Camille's. Although if I stole all her stuff and left her with my inside-out umbrella, that would be pretty funny. But I don't want all her stupid junk. What I want, and all I need, is a Hefty sack. A hole for my head, holes for my arms, and *ta-da,* I've got a poncho. Plus, it rolls up to nothing and I can tuck it in my backpack, no problem.

So that's all I need, although right now I've got to tell you—

I'm thinking a lot about food. You already know what happened at breakfast, lunch never arrived, and for dinner Mrs. Bender said through the door, "Howie told me what you did today, and I'm sorry, but you're going to have to learn that that sort of behavior is just not acceptable in this household. There'll be no supper for you tonight."

Who knows what he told her, but I know what they had for dinner—pot roast. I could smell it. Pot roast with whipped potatoes and, I think, buttered carrots. And probably some pie for dessert. They always have pie for dessert.

I could hear their utensils clinking. I could hear their voices going back and forth. The whole time they were eating, my stomach gurgled and grumbled and growled. My mouth watered and I wanted to beat on the door and beg for a plate. I wanted to break down and say, "I'm sorry! I promise I'll be good!"

But I didn't.

I didn't, and I won't.

I can still taste the Sani-Flush in my mouth. Still hear the water rushing into my ears. Still feel Mr. Bender's hand ripping my hair and crushing my face.

Tomorrow I'm out of here.

Hefty sack or not, I'm out of here.

Monday, May 24th

I actually almost told you, you know that? I actually almost told you why my eyes were so red. Not from crying, like you thought. From Sani-Flush water.

And then you whispered, "Have you tried journaling?" and I actually almost told you, Yes! And it helps about as much as a hammer to the head!

And then, when you asked if there was anything you could do, I actually almost said, Believe! That's what you can do! Believe me when I tell you about Mr. Bender and the laundry room and the Sani-Flushing.

But of course you wouldn't have. Or if you did, you'd think you were doing something by, wow, calling social services. Then they'd "investigate" and discover that I'm a liar and a thief and a drug user.

Ooh. Big help.

So I didn't tell you.

Now quit pretending to care.

ALMOST
(an official poem, which came to mind
after reading what I wrote above)

You asked me why my eyes were red,
I actually almost told you.
You asked if I'd been journaling,
I actually almost told you.
You asked me what the matter was,
I actually almost told you.
But instead
I said
"Kiss off!"

Crud. I feel kind of bad now. Maybe I should have told you.
Running away does scare me.

Still Monday, lunchtime

I am ready! I've scored so much stuff! Lost-and-found is a gold mine! There was even money in it! First I found a couple of quarters in a jacket I tried on, then I searched *all* the pockets of *everything.* Kids have way too much stuff, you know that? They lose all sorts of things that they don't even miss. Why? Because they've got so much *other* stuff to take its place. Me, if I lose my jacket, I know it. *Brrrrrrr,* do I know it! But in lost-and-found there's money, jewelry, purses, hair bands, shoes, jackets, sweaters, scarves, blankies, *backpacks.* . . . How can you lose your backpack and not go look in lost-and-found? What do you have, another one as a backup? Just in case? Does your mommy go out and buy you a new one because you lost your old one?

What kind of life is that?

Backup backpacks.

Whatever. What I was saying was, I scored big-time. I found an awesome jacket. Way better than mine. It's so great that I even wrote my name on the tag in case someone sees me with it and says it's theirs.

I also found mittens, a ski scarf, a ball cap, a working *watch,* and a whopping ten dollars and seventeen cents! Then I went to the janitor's room and scored not one, but two Hefty sacks (with those you can *use* a backup!). And excuse me, but while I was at it, I dug around and found a box cutter, a lighter, some twine, and a flashlight. It's an awesome flashlight, too. Small but powerful.

So now my backpack's got stolen goods *and* a weapon. Here's your chance to expel me!

Bring it on!

Like I'm coming back anyway.

Monday, last recess

You made me lie to you again, but how stupid can you be? Camille didn't tell you that I ate food out of the trash because she was concerned. She told you because she thinks I'm disgusting.

And yeah, the truth is that I did fish food out of the trash. I'd eaten all my own lunch because I was, big surprise here, *hungry*. But I wanted to stash away some food so I don't have to break into my ten dollars and seventeen cents tonight, and the chicken nuggets that Camille and her stupid friends threw away were perfectly good. I'm sorry they saw me, but come on, what's the big deal? You don't get all worried when someone pulls a sweatshirt from the lost-and-found, right? Food in the trash is like the *tossed*-and-found.

Besides, as my mom used to say, it was above the rim.

Monday, 3:17 p.m.

So this is it. I'm on the school bus like I'm supposed to be, but we just passed my stop. Good riddance, Benders! Sayonara, snake-breath! Adios, bozos! I'll miss you like a nightmare.

Oh. I just remembered.

Blackie.

Oh, crud.

I wish I could take him with me. . . .

Still Monday, 10:30 p.m.

I'm sitting in a booth in a fast food joint, chowing down on some of Camille's chicken nuggets, rounded out with salad bar freebies. They're not supposed to be freebies, but no one's going to hassle me for snagging a little supplemental nutrition, right? People do it all the time.

I love the croutons, *mm-mmm*. And don't worry, I'm balancing things out with some pineapple chunks and even some of that mixed bean stuff that all salad bars have but nobody likes. You know what I'm talking about—red beans, tan beans, onions, vinegar. My mom always made me eat it, so that's why I'm doing it now.

So where am I?

You're not going to believe this, but I made it over the state line. In one day! I have totally escaped!

This is what I did: I took the school bus to the farthest stop, found a city bus stop, figured out the map, told a lady who was waiting at the stop that I'd lost my money and didn't know what to do. She bought me a ticket, and I just stayed on that bus until it turned north, then I got off.

So, okay, I'll interrupt myself to tell you that I do have a destination.

West.

I don't care *where* west, just somewhere warm. So southwest, I guess. It's hard being homeless in the snow, okay? I'm not doing that again.

Oh, and one more thing—I've decided I'm *not* homeless.

I'm a gypsy. I'm a gypsy and my home is the great outdoors.

Hmm. I wonder if I could get to Hawaii somehow. It would be fun to be a sea gypsy! I'd live down by the ocean and eat coconuts and pineapples and mangoes. And I'd go swimming with the dolphins. Or I'd go swimming with other sea gypsies. That'd be so much fun! A bunch of gypsy kids riding waves, laughing, and playing in the surf. And afterward we'd build a big bonfire and roast fish that we caught in a big net that we made out of seaweed, and we'd tell stories all night and just sleep there by the fire and look up at the stars.

Yeah, it'd be great to be a gypsy in Hawaii.

I wonder what kind of dogs they have there. . . .

Thinking about Hawaii has made me hungry for more pineapple. I'll be right back. . . .

The manager gave me the evil eye, but what do I care? I smiled and took the pineapple anyway. He's not even close to kicking me out. There's a group of goth kids in the back booth that he's a lot more annoyed with.

Anyway, after I got off the city bus, I went across the street and used the bathroom at a gas station, then went inside the station's minimart thinking I'd try and lift a map. If I don't know where I'm going, I might wind up back where I started, right? That would be bad, bad news. And stupid, too!

So while I was pocketing a map, I overheard a man say *this* into his cell phone as he picked out a bottle of Mountain Dew and a bag of pretzels: "No, I'm just going straight through. I'll drop Shooting Star in Aaronville, then come on home. . . . That'd be nice, hon. . . . Uh-huh . . . uh-huh . . . don't worry, I'll be fine."

I'd seen a horse trailer hitched to a truck out in the gas lanes, and Shooting Star sure sounded like the name of a horse to me. Plus, the guy was wearing cowboy boots.

So I beat it outside, hid around the corner, looked up Aaronville in the map's index, and when I saw that it was due west, I got real excited.

Just so you know, I have a rule that I stick to:

I don't hitchhike.

Ever.

But that rule does not apply to stowing away!

Hey, the Stowaway Gypsy, that's who I am! You don't want to leave your trailer unlocked around me! I'll hop inside, and I'll take a ride.

Hmm. That's got a little rhythm. Like a poem. Or maybe a rap. Why didn't you include rapping in your handy-dandy poetry sheet, anyway? You don't think it's real poetry? No . . . what do you call them . . . ? Oh yeah, *iambic pentameters.*

Well, check this out:

I'm the Stowaway Gypsy and I need a ride
I'm gettin' in your trailer and I'm gonna hide
I'm snoozin' and cruisin' and havin' a rest
While Shootin' Star and me get chauffeured out WEST

I actually laughed out loud just now. The goth kids even looked over. But hey, let 'em glare. That was fun.

Anyway, I was going to tell you that I didn't exactly ride *with* Shooting Star—the door was locked. But as I was hurrying around the trailer looking for a window I could climb through, I saw another door near the front of the trailer, and it was *un*locked.

The truck fired up, so I opened the door quick and hopped inside. And do you know where I wound up?

Inside a cowboy changing room! That's what it seemed to be, anyway. It was amazing! It was totally walled off from the horse stalls and had all sorts of cowboy clothes hanging on hooks and poles and just kicking around. Shirts, hats, gloves, boots . . . that sort of stuff. There was also tack gear or whatever you call the stuff they put on horses. Saddles, ropes, bits or bites or, you know—horse stuff. The floor was metal, which would have made for a long, hard ride, but there was a fat stack of horse blankets under the rack of clothes. I couldn't believe my luck! As soon as we were onto the interstate, I made myself a mat of blankets, lay down, and just conked out.

I've learned that you should sleep when you can. There are a couple of reasons for this: Your body temperature drops when you sleep, and if you're stuck on the streets in the cold and you're so tired that you fall asleep, you can freeze to death.

Another reason is, people don't like homeless people sleeping on their property. They're afraid they're going to burn the place down with their cigarettes or steal their stuff or pee on their posies or something. I can't really blame them because I've known a lot of homeless people, and yeah, most of them would pee on your posies.

Do you have posies, Ms. Leone?

I don't even know what they are, to tell you the truth. Some kind of flower, I think. Like a pansy? Mom used to sing that old kids' song. She sang real airy. Real dreamy.

"Ring around the rosy
A pocket full of posies
Ashes, ashes,
We all fall down."

It took me a long time to figure out she sang like that when she was high.

It took me even longer to understand that the song's about death.

Is it a song, Ms. Leone? Or is it a poem?

I guess it doesn't matter.
It's still about death.

Tuesday, May 25th

This journal is helping me remember what day it is. Because you know what? When you're a gypsy, you lose track. Like right now it feels like a week ago that I ran away, but it's been less than 24 hours.

And I know I didn't finish telling you about sneaking *out* of the trailer and all that, but I got so bummed thinking about my mother that I just didn't want to write anymore. I shouldn't talk about her at all. It always makes me want to throw things.

Or cry.

Besides, right after I wrote that stuff about "Ring Around the Rosy," the manager caught the goth kids drinking from a flask and

26

kicked them out. And I could tell he was on his way over to kick *me* out, so I just packed up quick and split.

It was after midnight, anyway.

I just realized something. I wrote in this journal for almost two hours straight last night. That's crazy! Why am I writing, which I hate to do, to someone I don't like and will never see again?

Why?

I'm just killing time, that's all. So don't get it in your head that I *like* doing this. I'd way rather be reading a book. I love books. Or what I *should* be doing is reading the weather section of the newspaper. When you're a gypsy, you've got to know about the weather. It's one of your main survival tools. You need it to plan the day, and especially the night.

I was cold last night, and today it's cloudy and I'm afraid it might rain. Plus, I've got to figure out exactly where I am so I can figure out how to get *out* of here. Although if it's not going to rain, I might just take the day off from traveling, because despite the cold I actually slept okay last night. I put on everything and wrapped myself in the horse blanket that I snagged when I left the trailer. Then I slipped inside a Hefty sack to keep the dew off of me, and nestled in some bushes behind a building that's about a quarter of a mile from the fast food joint. There were no animals rustling around, no people bugging me . . . it worked out okay. Last night I thought the building was an old folks' home, but it turns out it's the *library*.

Same difference if you ask me.

Oh, lighten up, Ms. Leone. If you paid attention at all, you know I love the library. Where else can a person like me get books? But you have to admit old people use public libraries a lot more than young people.

Excuse me, not old people, *seniors.*

They're seniors and I'm a gypsy.

I'm a pretty hungry gypsy, actually. So I'm going to eat the rest of my cafeteria stash, then head over to the library and snag a book. (I'm sick of writing in this one.) So chow for now!

(Actually, now I'm remembering that the goodbye *chow* isn't spelled that way. It's *ciao* or something weird like that. It's Italian, right? But I'm not an Italian gypsy, I'm a hungry gypsy. So spelling it *chow* makes total sense.)

Still Tuesday, 9:30 a.m.

The library doesn't open until *noon,* can you believe that? The clouds are clearing and it looks like the perfect day to hang around outside and read a book. But I won't be able to get my hands on one until *noon.*

Stupid library.

11:30 a.m.

I tried fishing a book out of the night return, but they make the slide thing so your arm can't bend around it. I also walked around town for a while, but mostly what I've been doing is reading this stupid journal. It's weird to read your own writing, you know that? It's embarrassing.

And okay. I've been sitting here thinking a long time about whether to say this or not, but what the heck. Here goes:

You know "Almost"? My first official poem that I wrote a few pages back? And you know how before the poem there's the explanation of what happened? Well, I think "Almost" explains it better than the explanation.

At least it makes me *feel* it better.

Something about that really bothers me.

10:30 at night

I've got to get out of Aaronville. This is a podunk little town, and I swear everybody's giving me the who-are-you-and-where's-your-mother look.

Dead, you morons! Dead!

I hate that look because it reminds me.

Plus, it usually means the police'll come sniffing around.

So, Holly, you ask, it's ten-thirty at night . . . are you back in the bushes?

Are you crazy? Am I wasting battery power writing this with my flashlight on?

No chance!

Or as my mother would say, "No chance in France!"

She always wanted to go to France. And when she talked about it, she'd always wind up singing some song about breaking through to the other side.

29

Break on through to the other side,

Break on through to the other side . . .

Have you ever heard that song? There were more words, but that's all I remember.

Crud. I've got to stop talking about my mom. What I was telling you about is where I am, which is inside Aaronville's *other* fast food joint. There's no salad bar here, but when I scoped out the place where I went last night, that same manager guy was walking around the dining area, so I came here instead.

That's the pain about being a gypsy child instead of a gypsy adult. People call the cops a lot quicker.

But it turns out that this place has a great dollar menu. And since I was all out of Camille's cafeteria food, I broke down and spent my first buck. I ordered a double cheeseburger, and when I asked if veggies were extra, the girl who rang me up said, "Nah." So I asked for pickles and onions and lettuce and tomatoes. "Lots!" I told her.

She looked at me like I was a dweeb, and when my burger arrived, it had about six inches of veggies on it. I suspect they were making fun of me, because the place is pretty dead and they don't seem to have much to do, but the joke's on them. I took all the veggies off, got a little plastic fork and knife and a few mayo packets, cut the mayo into the veggies, tossed it all with salt and pepper, and *mm-mmm.* One delicious *free* salad.

So I'm down a dollar, but I still have half the burger, which I'll save for breakfast. It's cold enough outside to keep it from rotting, but I hope it doesn't attract bears. Though I doubt there are bears in

30

Aaronville. Dogs, sure. But if one of them comes sniffing around, I'll share.

So you want to know what I did all day?

Well, I'm not going to go into a ton of detail because I don't want to waste my whole night writing again, but basically, I went into the library, where I used the bathroom, read the paper, got quizzed up by a librarian (I told her I was homeschooled and that I was doing an assignment), "borrowed" a paperback book that looked pretty good (but wasn't), read the whole thing out in the sunshine at a park (which was really more like a strip mall of grass), walked to the outskirts of town, and discovered (*ta-da*) train tracks!

And guess what?

They run east-west!

Oh, crud. Those same goth kids from last night just came in and spotted me.

They're looking at me and whispering.

And evil-goth-kid laughing.

I'm out of here.

May 26ᵗʰ, 10 a.m.

There are probably only four goth kids in this whole podunk town, and of course their idea of fun is terrorizing the town's only gypsy. Too bad for them I've got a lot of experience ditching people: goth kids, cops, store managers, pizza delivery boys. . . . The way I do it is, I cut and run, then I hide and hold.

It's the "holding" part that's hard. Even five minutes of holding still seems like an eternity, but you've got to make yourself do it for at *least* half an hour. It's the key to getting away. If you come out too early, you'll get caught, guaranteed.

The goth kids were plenty ticked off when I lost them. I could hear them shouting at each other, "She went this way!" "No, dude, *this* way!"

I held still for like an *hour* before finally going back to the library bushes, but the whole thing made me jumpy. I didn't sleep very well at all. I woke up about twenty times.

And since I'd already overstayed my unwelcome in Aaronville, I packed up early this morning, ate my half-a-burger, and hiked down to the town's 7-Eleven, which I'd walked past the day before.

I waited for the prework rush, when all 7-Elevens (even the one in Aaronville) get busy. I had a mental list already made: pop-top cans of meat, protein bars, and Gatorade. No filler food like candy and cookies—Spam will take you a lot farther than Oreos.

I'm sure you've noticed that 7-Elevens have shoplifting mirrors and cameras everywhere, but I've learned about timing and positioning and how to avoid getting caught. And in all the food runs I've made (which I'm sure you'll be horrified to learn is way more than I can remember), I've only been busted once.

I bit my way out of that one.

Anyway, I went into the 7-Eleven, keeping the rules of lifting in the front of my mind: Find the mirrors. Find the employees. Act normal. Don't linger. Don't dart your eyes around. Don't get greedy. Be smooth.

I also attached myself to an adult, without getting so close that she noticed. She made for great cover as I slipped things into my jacket pockets.

The last rule is: Buy something. You've got to, or why'd you come in?

So I stood in line with all the rush-hour people and bought myself a pack of gum. Sugar-free peppermint. When you run out of food, it really helps with the hunger pangs.

Then I walked out and hiked to the outskirts of town, and now I'm down at the railroad tracks.

Waiting.

May 28th (2 long days later)

Hollywood movies are stupid. They make it look like *anyone* could jump on a train, but that's a lie, you hear me? A stupid, romanticized lie.

Probably like Hollywood itself, now that I think about it.

Which, by the way, is the *last* place I want to wind up.

Who wants to be homeless in Hollywood?

But forget that. I don't want to talk about Hollywood. I want to talk about reality. Reality is, you don't just hop on a train. Reality is, you can *kill* yourself trying, which is something I found out the hard way.

I'd been waiting the whole day for a train to come by because it's not like I had a train *schedule* or anything. There's no depot or switching yard or whatever in Aaronville. There's just a track that cuts around the south end of town.

So when I finally heard a rumble in the distance, I'm all, Okay! Here comes the train!

I'd found a place I thought would be good for swinging on board, and I was chomping at the bit to do it. The train sounded just like a train's supposed to: *chuga*-chuga-*chuga*-chuga-*chuga*-chuga-*chuga*-chuga. . . . And once or twice the whistle would blow: *woo-woooo!*

I was stoked!

But the closer it got, the louder it got and the bigger and heavier and *deadlier* it seemed.

I still jumped out from my hiding place and ran toward the train as the locomotive blasted by. But I couldn't run fast enough, I couldn't grab high enough. I tried over and over again, but the cars kept barreling by. The train was so loud. So big. So *fast.* And then I tripped on one of the railroad ties and almost landed *under* the train.

It was the scariest thing I've ever done (and that's saying something!). I crawled away from the tracks, and when the train had thundered by, I just sat on the ground, shaking.

I probably sat there for a whole hour, shaking. I thought about going back into town, but I didn't want to push my luck. Little towns are full of busybodies, and I'd already hung around too long. So when I finally quit shaking, I got up and started following the railroad tracks west.

I can hear you now: Holly! What were you *thinking*?

So here's what I was thinking: To the west are hills. Hills mean *up*hill. Uphill means the train will slow down. A slower train means the Stowaway Gypsy can get on board.

It seemed like a pretty good plan.

At the time.

I walked along the tracks until it was almost dark, eating and (especially) drinking as little as I could stand.

No train came by the whole rest of the day. The temperature dropped quick after the sun was down, and since I'd been walking and sweating, *I* got cold quick when I stopped to make camp.

I wasn't sure what kinds of animals were lurking around, hoping to sink their teeth into tired gypsy meat, so I climbed up to an isolated ledge on a big rock formation. I decided that yeah, I'd be pretty safe up there, so I collected a little arsenal of rocks, left them on the ledge, then climbed down and gathered wood for a fire.

Fire is what saved the caveman, you know that? If it wasn't for fire, the human race would have died off ages ago. We're wimps! We've got no fur, we've got no fangs . . . but we've got fire. And for your information, Ms. Leone, the crumpled pages of a lousy novel make a great fire starter. I'm telling you this because I think if you were ever stuck out in the woods overnight, you'd probably have a book with you. You told us over and over that you don't think you could *live* without books, but the ironic thing is, you'd probably *die* before you'd think to rip the pages out of one to start a fire. Am I right?

Well, get over it already. Better to be warm than well-read.

It took about twenty pages to get the little twigs going, and once they were burning, the bigger sticks dried out and caught fire, too.

I didn't just use the fire to warm up. I used it to dry the sweat from my clothes, especially my socks. (Sweaty socks make your feet *freeze* at night. Ooh, it's miserable.) I also used it to burn a Vienna sausages can clean. I guess I could have dumped the can a ways away (so

35

the smell wouldn't lead animals to me), but my mother and I always burned cans out. You can use them afterward for cups or scoops if you have to.

I really wanted to open the can of Spam I'd lifted because I was still hungry, but I ate the second half of a protein bar instead and washed it down with two sips of Gatorade. (Two sips is so hard when you're dying of thirst and there's no one to stop you, but my Gatorade was more than half gone, so I forced myself to stop drinking.)

Then I put on every stitch of clothing I had, and when the fire died out, I climbed up to my ledge and went to bed, with rocks at the ready and the flashlight in my hand. Animals don't like light in their eyes, and that plus zinging rocks is the quickest way to get them to back off.

I didn't sleep very well at all. I kept waking up from animal noises—rustling, flapping wings, howling—but I didn't actually come face to face with any gypsy killers.

It was still dark when I gave up trying to get back to sleep. I was dying of thirst, my hips were sore, and the bottom half of me was freezing! But when the sky started getting light, I saw that my Hefty sack was dripping with dew. I licked it like crazy, and when I couldn't reach any more, I eased out of the sack, held the edges to make a trough, then ran the dew into my mouth.

I probably got only three or four tablespoons total, but it made me feel great! So I packed up and started hiking west along the tracks again. They had to go somewhere, right? And they *were* going uphill. But from sunrise to sunset I hiked along the tracks, sweating liquids I couldn't afford to lose, burning energy I didn't have enough food to re-place. And how many trains came by?

None.

I finally made camp again, went through the same routine again, woke up hungrier and thirstier than ever, got up and started hiking again. My whole body was sore. I felt hungry and tired and weak, but I kept walking.

Kept . . . on . . . walking.

Finally, *finally,* I heard a rumble. At first I was ecstatic, but then I panicked. I was in a terrible place to try to hop on! I'd trip again! I'd probably fall under the wheel and *splat,* it'd be all over. Maybe I should just keep walking! Maybe there was a town up ahead with a switching yard where I could just climb on.

But I was in the middle of nowhere, with very little food and even less water, and I had seen no glow of city lights in the distance the night before. The next town might be days away. I didn't really have a choice. I had to try.

The rumbling was getting louder, but I didn't see the train. I was running along the tracks, trying to find a good spot where the ties weren't so uneven, strapping my backpack down tight, looking over my shoulder, telling myself I could do this, I could do this, I could, I could. . . .

But where was the train?

Then it came blasting around the curve in *front* of me, barreling east.

Woo-woooo, the whistle blasted. *Woo-woooo.*

I about shot out of my pants. And as I scrambled away, the whistle blasted long and hard, which makes me think the engineer saw me.

It took me a little while to recover from *that* heart attack, and then

I got really depressed. If a train only came by every other day, and half those days it was going in the wrong direction, how was I ever going to catch it?

There was nothing to do but keep walking. And since the train was cutting through the hills now, and since the track was real tight between cliffs in places, I had to climb up the side of the hill (which felt more like a *mountain*). It took me most of the day, but when I reached the top, I had an amazing view to the north and to the west.

Could I see cities? Towns? Villages? Tepees?

Nope. Just trees and rocks and train tracks, going on forever and ever.

I stuck a piece of gum in my mouth and headed down the other side, and that's where I am now.

So, you ask, are you writing this on your deathbed? Is it your last desperate act before going to the Great Beyond?

My last desperate act *journaling*?

Get real, Ms. Leone.

No, I'm writing this from the comfort of a blackberry patch. A blackberry patch by a creek. The blackberries are sour (they're more like redberries), but the water is so sweet. It is the best water I have ever, ever, *ever* tasted.

And you want to know what the best thing of all is?

Right around the corner there's a ledge that has a tree growing on it, and that tree has a branch that hangs over the tracks!

I'd say it's twenty feet above the tracks, which looks like a long way down, but think about it this way: A train car is about ten feet tall. (I think it's actually more than that. Wheels and all? Definitely more than that. But we'll just say ten.) And dangling by my arms from a branch, I'm about six feet long. (From hand to toe? Yeah, it's probably about six.) That means that the drop to the top of a train car will only be about four feet.

Anyone can do that, right?

Four little feet.

I'm not even going to think about missing. I'm not even going to think about how fast the train'll be going and how hard I'm going to land. I'm going to stay here eating sour berries until the train comes by, and then I'm just going to do it.

Do it or die.

May 29ᵗʰ, 9:00 a.m.

Bad thought: I think it's Saturday. And a holiday weekend. What if trains don't run on holiday weekends?

I don't know how long I can live on sour berries. . . .

May 29ᵗʰ, 3:00 p.m.

It was about 11:00 this morning, and I had just filled my Gatorade bottle with water again when I heard the rumble, way off in the distance. "Yay!" I shouted. "They're running!" And I packed everything up quick.

Trains make an awesome rumble. It's ferocious but musical. If they just chug-chugged, they'd be only ferocious. But they *chuga*-chuga, and it changes everything. It turns a train from a ferocious iron beast to a ferocious iron beast with a song in its heart.

Anyway, I went over to the tree, shinnied about halfway out on the branch, and then you know what I did?

I totally panicked.

This was crazy! I was up way too high! It could not be done! I'd *die.*

Have you ever been twenty feet up in the air over railroad tracks? You'd mess your shorts bad, Ms. Leone, honest you would.

But I made myself take a deep breath and I told myself, "You can do this. You can do this. . . . You can do this, you can do this. . . ." And then words started chugging through my brain in rhythm with the train:

Chuga-chuga, chuga-chuga . . . (You can do this, you can do this.)

Chuga-chuga, chuga-chuga . . . (You can do this, you can do this!)

I looked back and forth, waiting. I couldn't tell which direction the train was coming from.

Then it rounded the bend.

It was westbound!

You can do this, you can do this.

The train was chugging slower than before. Much slower!

But the closer it got, the *faster* it seemed to be going.

You can do this, you can do this.

I scooted out farther on the branch. The whole tree shook as the locomotive approached and passed underneath me.

You can do this, you can do this.

This was it. It was time!

I swung my leg around. I lowered myself until I was hanging from the branch.

You can do this, you can do this.

But the cars weren't the open-bin kind. They were flatcars with logs and bricks and pipes.

I couldn't land on those!

You can do this, you can do this.

More bricks, more pipes, more logs. I hung there for an eternity. My arms were aching.

You can do this, you can do this.

No, I can't! It's too far down! There's nothing to land on!

You can do this, you can do this!

The whole train's passing me by!

You can do this, you can do this. . . .

I can't hold myself like this much longer! I'm going to die!

And then I saw something.

Potatoes?

Yes! Three cars of potatoes!

You can do this, you can do this. . . .

The first potato car was under me, under me, under me, gone.

You can do this, you can do this. . . .

The second one was under me, under me, under me, gone!

Do it, Holly—do it, Holly—do it, Holly, then the whistle blew, *DOOOOOO-IT!*

And I did.

Don't think it was like landing on marshmallows, Ms. Leone. I landed *hard,* then catapulted forward and slammed into the rear of the car.

I think I passed out for a minute, and I could barely move my arm for about five. So it'd be a lie to say that I'm not battered and bruised, but hey, nothing's broken. And now here I am, safe and sound on a mountain of potatoes, getting a free ride west.

Woo-woooo!

June 8th

I can't believe it's June 8th. I was wiped out for over a week? I must have eaten too many potatoes. Or maybe it was the berries. My stomach was cramping so hard that I could barely walk. And my bruises were so tender and looked *so* bad. Then I got a fever, and I don't know, I've just been wiped out.

Maybe it's not really June 8th. The people here lie about everything. Although they were nice to let me camp with them. There are four of them living under this bridge near the switching yard where I got off the train. They've been pretty nice about food, too. After I could eat again, they started giving me their leftovers. I even got some lasagna from this old guy, Frankie, today. It was actually still a little bit warm.

Next day (so I guess that's June 9th)

Frankie says I've got to help him panhandle today. Says he'll get way more money if there's a kid with him.

Says I owe him for the lasagna.

7:00 p.m.

I hate panhandling. It's humiliating, but I hate it doubly because of the law. If I'm doing it on my own, the cops'll haul me over to social services. If I'm doing it with a "parent," that's okay.

Frankie scored over a hundred bucks today. He gave me twenty.

From now on I'll buy my own lasagna.

June 10th

Frankie tried to steal the twenty bucks back last night when he thought I was sleeping. I elbowed him in the face, which made him curse and say, "I did all the work! All you did was sit there!"

He was slurring and staggering and looked like he was going to kick me, but instead he stumbled down the embankment and passed out.

It didn't take long for the others to swoop in and pick his pockets clean.

The creeps.

June 11th

One of the women that's staying under this bridge keeps asking me what I'm writing in. For some reason she thinks I'm a narc. Every time I open this journal she screeches, "The narc's at it again!"

Oh, brother, there she goes again.

Okay, I just shouted back, "I'm not a narc! I'm just writing in a journal!"

She screeched, "A *journal*?" Then one of the other women yelled, "Homeless don't write in journals! We want to forget this life, not write about it!"

"I'm not homeless," I shouted back. "I'm a gypsy!"

Well, stupid me. You should see them now. They're all huddled up arguing like crazy. Maybe they think I'm going to put a curse on them.

I can't believe it. They're coming up here?

Oh, crud. Frankie's got a stick.

June 12th

It really is June 12th. I saw a newspaper stand at a gas station where I used the bathroom. Pukiest bathroom I've ever been in. I should've found some bushes.

But forget that. The thing about it being June 12th is that it's *Saturday,* June 12th, which means the last day of school came and went and I didn't even know it.

Before I ran away, I used to think about the last day of school all the time because I *didn't* want it to come. Not because I'd miss you or my stupid classmates. I didn't want school to end because I knew it would mean having to deal with the Benders more, no seeing Blackie, and longer laundry-room lockdowns. But now that I'm gone and I'm not worried about those things, I can't help wondering what the last day of school was like. Did you have a big stupid end-of-the-year-have-a-great-summer party?

I'm sure you did. You're the kind who would. I can just see you welling with tears, telling all the kids, "You were such a special class! I'll miss you! I'll miss you! I'll miss you!"

Admit it—you say that every year, and every year you close the door and forget about them.

Same way, I'm sure, you've forgotten about me.

Saturday, 10:30 a.m.

It's bugging me that I can't forget about *you.* Why do I keep writing to you like you can hear me? How many times have I told myself that I'm through writing in this journal? Then I pick it up and write some more.

45

Okay, this is stupid but I'm saying it anyway because sometimes when I say things "out loud," I can tell whether they're true or not. Don't ask me why that's so, it just is.

So here it is. Here's the reason I might keep thinking about you:

Maybe I was too mean to you.

Maybe you really did care.

Oh, crud. Why am I crying?

I hate myself for believing that.

Even if it's just a little.

Still Saturday, 3:00 p.m.

Okay. The *real* reason I'm writing in this is because I'm bored. You got that? Bored. And here's proof of just how bored I am:

I read your handy-dandy poetry sheet like ten times today.

See?

I'm B-O-R-E-D!

So don't think that I believe any of the stuff I said before, because I don't.

By the way, it may surprise you to know that I've had a spectacular day. Once I got away from Frankie and escaped into downtown, I discovered that this is a great city! It's no podunk Aaronville, population 500 busybodies, that's for sure. I'm not going to tell you which city it is because I've been thinking that if this gets into the wrong hands, that could spell really bad news. You think I want social services tracking me down? No chance! No chance in France!

Anyway, what was I saying?

Oh, yeah. My spectacular day.

It took me a while to get my bearings straight, but when I did, I found a big park with miles of grass and willowy trees and daffodils or daisies or, you know, happy little flowers everywhere. It also has a lake with birds galore, and a footpath that goes around the water. And if that description doesn't make you say, Ah, lovely! wait until you hear what I did all day.

I watched the Parade of Dogs!

It wasn't an official parade, but I swear everybody in town with a dog came out to the park today to go for a stroll. There were so many dogs that I even pretended I was a judge at the Westminster Dog Show. My favorite breed is mutt, by the way. If I was in charge of the Westminster Dog Show, I'd have a mutt category. Maybe I'd call it Magnificent Mutts to give it some dignity or whatever, but I'd open up a category for mutts and I'd judge on friendliness. Mutts would win Best of Show every year.

Anyway, here's the kind of great day I had: Not one person gave me The Look. They let me pet their dogs, they were friendly and patient, and no one acted like, I really don't have *time* to let you see my dog, or even said, Uh . . . where's your mother?

So it's been a happy, relaxing day, and sleeping here last night was great, but you know what? I need a shower. I need a shower *bad*. I'm keeping my hair under my hat, which I'd do anyway because it helps me look like a boy, but right now I've got it under my hat because I can't stand having it loose. It's just too gross.

The other thing that I need is a toothbrush. If I don't want to end up *looking* like a homeless person, I've got to get my hands on a toothbrush. Toothpaste would be nice, too.

And a change of clothes.

Especially underwear.

(Don't wrinkle your nose. They don't exactly have laundry machines under bridges, you know.)

So this is what I'm thinking: There's a shelter in this city and I need to get inside it. I don't like homeless shelters because every one I've ever been in is depressing.

Besides, I don't belong in a homeless shelter.

I'm a gypsy.

But I can't even get into shelters anymore because I'm a "minor without a parent." I tried to sneak into four different shelters after I ran away from the Fisks. "Out," they all told me. "You can't be in here."

I even said, "Don't worry, my mom said to meet her here," but every time they just pointed to the door and said, "Until she shows up, you've got to get out." They made me feel like a mouse begging for crumbs. But instead of giving me food they set traps, which is how social services caught me and how I got stuck at the Benders'.

I've got to face facts, though: I may be a gypsy, but I'm a really gross gypsy, and a warm meal, a shower, a toothbrush, and a change of clothes sounds wonderful.

I've got to figure out a way to get inside.

Still Saturday, still the 12ᵗʰ, 9:30 p.m.

I found a new "mother." She's a homeless hag with no front teeth that I spotted at the bus station. She looks eighty but according to her ID, she's Louise K. Palmer, and she's only forty-eight.

She's got definite mental problems, which I could tell from across the station. She was squatting in a corner, one hand clutching the handle of a little two-wheeled metal basket of junk. Her eyes were closed and she was singing a song about Jesus loving the little people.

She sounded like a strangled bullfrog.

When I thought the time was right, I went up to her and asked, "Mom?"

She opened her eyes, then blinked at me a whole bunch. "Lisa? Oh, Lisa! I've been praying that you'd come!"

At first I felt horrible. Did she have a long-lost daughter named Lisa? Did losing Lisa make her crazy?

But then she blinked again and said, "Wait. You're Linda, aren't you." She cocked her head to the side. "Linda?"

"Uh, no," I said, then picked the most far-fetched name I could think of, just to make sure she hadn't had *two* daughters who'd maybe died in a horrible fire or something. "I'm Gigi, remember?"

"Oh, Gigi!" she said. "It's wonderful that you're here!" She had a state ID hanging from a lanyard around her neck, which I was happy to see. Some shelters will cut adults slack if they tell them their ID got stolen, but it's a lot less hassle to just show the ID and sign in.

And, believe this or not, kids don't need an ID if they're with a "parent."

So she was it. My ticket into the shelter. I put out my hand to help her up and said, "Come on, Mom. We've got to get home before they lock us out."

"They'll lock us out?"

"Curfew, remember? We have to be home by six or they'll lock us out without supper."

"Oh," she said, then smiled and took my hand.

Sorry. I've been spacing out, watching Louise K. Palmer snore. We are inside the shelter and she's zonked out on the cot next to mine, looking like a big toothless baby.

The cots are just army cots with blankets. No mattress or anything. They're more comfortable than the ground, but not much. What I really don't like about this kind of cot is the metal bars on the sides. They make me claustrophobic.

But the good news is . . . I'm squeaky! Clean clothes, clean hair, clean teeth, clean body . . . I feel great!

Louise K. Palmer is also clean, which was no small job. That woman was *caked*. I had to scrub really hard to get the dirt off of her. It was layers of skin deep.

I got her a change of clothes from the donation box, and after she dressed, she asked me to comb out her hair. It's long, almost clear to her waist. So I said, "Sure," and after a good ten minutes of detangling, I was finally done.

"More," she whispered.

So I picked up the comb again and worked it a little longer.

"More," she whispered again after I stopped. Then she turned to me and smiled. "It feels so nice."

So I combed her hair over and over, from root to tip, just like my mom used to do for me. And you know what? I didn't mind. She didn't say a word, and I didn't say a word. I didn't think bad thoughts, either. Like how she was wasting my time, or how it wasn't fair that my mom would never comb out my hair again. I thought about her. About Louise K. Palmer. And I made up a little story in my head about who she was and where she came from. And while I was making up the story, I pretended that the comb was a magic comb, and that it was untangling all the knots of her life. All the things that had confused her and hurt her and made her crazy, my magic comb was pulling them out.

When I finally put the comb down, her hair was dry.

Louise K. Palmer thinks a mountain of white bread with a pound of margarine is supper. Well, I had news for her. I took her tray and said, "Forget it! You're not getting this until you eat some . . ." And then I remembered that she has no teeth. "Soup!"

"I don't like pea soup," she said.

"You're eating it," I told her, and got us two big steaming bowls of it.

Soup at most shelters is watery, but this was homemade split pea with big chunks of tender ham. It was so good. So thick and salty and delicious. I can't remember ever tasting anything quite like it, and Louise K. Palmer must've thought so, too, because she wound up eating three whole bowls.

Crud! They just called lights out and I haven't told you half of what I wanted to.

Plus, I'm not going to be able to sleep a wink tonight.

I hate shelters.

People coughing and snoring and hacking up who-knows-what.

It's a nightmare.

But I do have clean teeth.

Sunday, June 13th

I wanted to spend the day at the park, but Louise K. Palmer didn't. And since I haven't figured out a travel plan yet, I didn't want to blow it by leaving the shelter without her and not being able to get back inside. And the truth is, I wouldn't mind having some more pea soup tonight.

So we went over to the day center, which is right next door, did some assigned chores (which means I did both of ours) and hung out on the patio and in the yard all morning.

I wish I could see what was going on inside Louise K. Palmer's head because *something* is. Why else would she curtsy? She's a toothless old hag and she *curtsys*. She also says *Adieu!* or *Au revoir!* and gives a regal wave every time she leaves a room. *Every* time, every room.

The manager came up to me and asked me what her story was. Like it's any of her business? So I told her, "Please, I can't bear to talk about it."

She didn't quit, though. She said, "But you seem so healthy, and she's so—"

"Please!" I cried, doing a pretty good freak-out. "Don't make me talk about it!"

She's been eyeing me ever since. And I've seen her on the phone and at her computer a lot, too, which I keep telling myself is normal, but it doesn't *feel* normal.

Either I'm paranoid, or she's onto me.

Still the 13ᵗʰ, 8:30 p.m.

We're back at the night shelter. The manager was only around in the morning, so good riddance to her. And I spent the entire rest of the day out in the yard working on something I'm, as they say, *loath* to tell you about.

It actually started yesterday while I was combing out Louise's hair. Probably because I'd read your handy-dandy poetry sheet and that stupid example of a ballad kept looping through my brain.

I was trying to keep the whole thing in my head, but it got bigger and bigger. So I scrawled sections of it—wait a minute, wait a minute—I scrawled *stanzas* on napkins. (I can't believe I remembered that word! Wash my mouth! I'm learning the language of poetry!)

Anyway, it may be awful, I wouldn't know. (Although could it be any worse than the example on your handout? Who speaks with *'tis* and *thou* and *thee* anymore? Honestly, Ms. Leone, you need to update your sheet.)

But awful or not, here it is:

THE BALLAD OF LADY LOUISE

By a new moon was born a sweet baby, Louise,
So innocent, perfect, and precious was she!
She learned how to curtsy, say thank you and please,
The bonnie young baby Louise.

The girl, she grew quick and so did her hair,
It tumbled in ringlets right down to her chair!
"Oh my, but the lass is so lovely and fair,
We must call her Lady Louise."

Soon suitors came calling with chocolates so creamy,
She ate sweets and thought each young man was quite dreamy.
But a renegade boy is who made her all steamy,
That naughty young Lady Louise!

She ran off with him and the story turns sad,
For dashing or not, the boy was a cad!
And not at all ready to be a new dad,
He left our poor Lady Louise.

She blossomed into an enormous bouquet,
People gossiped and gasped, "She must be due any day!"
But triplets take room and were still months away,
The babies of Lady Louise.

When her children were born, they were instantly taken,
’Twas best all around, but were they mistaken?
For the void left her lost and terribly shaken,
The heartbroken Lady Louise.

Years wandering streets she would call out their names,
Her efforts were futile, were lost, all in vain.
Still it howls through the night on the wind of her pain,
The voice of poor Lady Louise.

Now the moon is half full and so is her head,
And many believe she’d be better off dead.
But she waits at the station and hopes to be fed,
The homeless old lady, Louise.

Well, I just read that over and you know what? You may hate it, but I kind of like it. Except that it’s sad. And I can’t believe I used *’Twas*. I had to, though. Nothing else fit.

Funny thing, too: I don’t know what Louise K. Palmer’s real story is, but in my mind now, that’s it.

I hope no one ever writes “The Ballad of Holly Janquell.”

Or if they do, that it’s funny. And full of sass.

Hey! “The Ballad of Gypsy Janquell” . . . that would be good!

There once was a gypsy so clever and spry
Your pockets she’d pick in the wink of an eye
And if asked the truth, she surely would lie,
The Gypsy of . . .

Well, crud. I can't think of a rhyme. And double crud because I can't believe I'm wasting my time *trying*. Like I haven't spent the whole day doing this? I'd better not start thinking in stanzas, you hear me? I would be really, really ticked off if I started thinking in stanzas.

Monday, June 14th, 5:00 a.m.

I can't sleep. This place is a nightmare. No one's allowed to smoke inside the shelter, but they all smoke *outside* all day, then hack up their smoky lungs all night. The air reeks. I feel like I'm breathing in death and disease.

So I've decided: I'm taking a shower, I'm packing my stuff, and after breakfast, Louise or not, I'm out of here. I probably won't be able to come back, but so what? I'll be good for another week. Maybe two. And Louise won't miss me. She doesn't even seem to know who I am half the time. Besides, that day-shelter manager's definitely got a bee in her britches where I'm concerned, and I don't want to push my luck.

7:30 a.m.

Diversionary tactic. Write in the journal. Look calm. Act normal. Don't make eye contact. . . .

Why?

There are cops here! They're cruising through the tables looking for someone.

Please not me, please not me, please not me . . .

7:45 a.m.

They just left. All they did was look and leave.

"Adieu! Au revoir!" Loony Louise croaked after them.

I'm not delaying this any longer. I'm grabbing some supplies and I'm out of here.

Tuesday, June 22nd

It's been over a week? Well, I guess I'm bored again, is why I'm writing. Not that I haven't *been* bored during the week, but I scored some books at the library, so that's been a lot more entertaining than writing in this thing.

I guess I'm also writing because I need to bounce some ideas around. Life in the park isn't as peachy as it was a week ago. I've been getting The Look from people who've seen me more than once, and they've stopped letting me near their dogs. Not that I've been hanging out in the same spot every day, but the park seems to be getting smaller by the minute.

I've also noticed cops cruising by a *lot.*

I keep having to hide.

It makes me very, very nervous.

So what am I going to do? I can't go back to the shelter, and I can't stay here much longer. I've either got to find someplace else to hang out or move on.

See? Just talking about it makes me know what I should do.

It's time to move on.

Wednesday morning (the 23rd)

So here I am at the bus depot, waiting. And you know what? I am totally freaked out. I was in the middle of figuring out the Greyhound schedule, because I've got a great plan to get a free ride and I wanted to make sure I stowed away on the right bus, when this guy came up to me and said, "Real sorry about your mother."

It was like a slug to the gut by a ghost. It hurt bad, but it also didn't feel real.

Nobody had to tell me this guy was homeless. Scraggly beard, hunched posture, missing teeth, sun-baked face—he had homeless written all over him.

But how could he know my mother? How could he be this far from home in the same bus station as me? How could he even recognize me? I'd changed a lot since my mom had died.

"She looked so peaceful," he said. "Like an angel."

She *had* looked peaceful.

Just like an angel.

Which had made it torture to let go of her. The police had had to pry me away.

So while I was thinking about that, the man pressed four dollars on me and whispered, "It ain't much, but I hope it helps."

I think I was in shock, but as he walked away it dawned on me that he wasn't talking about my mother.

He was talking about Louise.

I wanted to call out, "Wait! Are you *sure*? What happened?"

But I didn't.

I couldn't take knowing.

When he'd gone around the corner, I told myself, Get a grip, Holly! The guy's just demented. A schizo. An old meth-head. An Ecstasy casualty.

But in my gut I know that isn't so.

You know what? When I started writing this entry, I was totally freaked out. But right now I'm doing okay because I've decided that if Louise did die, she died happy. Clean hair, clean clothes, warm soup . . . And I can just picture her arriving at the pearly gates, curtsying for Saint Peter and saying, *Bonjour, monsieur!*

How could he refuse to let her in?

And you know what else? I've come up with a final stanza to her poem. Working on it felt better than crying. It felt . . . nice.

Are you ready?

Here it is:

> So comb out the knots of this tangly tale,
> For the angels have come and their ship's set to sail.
> They've got her on board looking peaceful and pale,
> *Adieu, au revoir,* sweet Louise.

Now if that lousy bus would show up, I might be able to blow this joint.

Wednesday night

Well, crud. I didn't have a prayer of a chance on the first west-bound bus. And I got thrown off the second one. It was so comfy inside, too! Tall, soft seats, plenty of room to stretch out . . . talk about the lap of luxury! Man, I wish I could buy a ticket.

But forget that. I bought a one-dollar double cheeseburger instead. And even though this McDonald's where I am is open 24 hours, I'm beat. I need to get some sleep.

But where?

I'm afraid to go back to the park because I'm sure the cops are on the lookout for me. Especially if Louise really is dead. I can just hear the conversation:

> *Cops:* I was told she had next of kin. A daughter?
>
> *Day Manager:* That girl wasn't her daughter. She just latched on to her for a free meal. I did some checking and found the girl's picture in the runaway database. Here's a copy.
>
> *Cops:* Thanks. You've been a big help.
>
> *Day Manager:* You need to find her so we can get her back into foster care.
>
> *Cops:* Will do.

I should have left a week ago.

I can't believe it. I'm actually thinking about going back to the bridge. It seems like a lifetime ago that Frankie chased me off with a stick. And what's weird is, right now being back at the bridge seems safer than staying in the park.

I do not want to get picked up by cops.

I'd way rather defend myself against a man with a stick than a social worker with good intentions.

Sunday, June 27th

I'm still in the same town and you're going to laugh, because you know where I've been living since Wednesday night?

A school!

I was heading for the park when I saw this SCHOOL crossing sign and thought, Hey, maybe I'll sleep at the school. It's summertime, right? The place will be deserted.

It turned out to be a high school, and it's *big*. After walking around awhile, trying all the doors, I spotted an open window on the back side of the gym. It was way up high, but right underneath it was this big storage cage they'd built for trash cans and other junk that I guess they don't want people messing with. So I climbed the cage, pulled the window open as far as it would go, and squeezed through.

I wound up in the girls' locker room, and you know what? It's perfect! There are mats to sleep on, showers with hot water, toilets that flush, and the gym teachers' office is *loaded* with stuff. Books, a radio, a TV that plays movies (which there's a whole shelf of!), a microwave (and popcorn to go with it!), a refrigerator (with yogurts, burritos, fruit cups, Cokes . . . yum!).

I could live the rest of my life here.

Monday, June 28th

I came into the office this morning and tidied up because my garbage was spread everywhere. And while I was doing that, you know what I found?

A phone.

It's one of those big ones with two hold buttons and a bunch of different lines. I found it stashed in a desk drawer, of all places.

At first I thought it was just an old dead phone, but when I pulled it out, there were cables attached, and when I held up the receiver and pushed the LINE 1 button, I got a dial tone.

So I've been sitting at this desk for the longest time, thinking. And it's really bummed me out, because of all the millions of people there are in this world, I have no one to call.

No one.

Still the 28th, 2:30 p.m.

I hate cheerleaders. I bet you were a cheerleader, huh, Ms. Leone? Popular, friendly, pretty, *enthusiastic.*

Yeah. You were a cheerleader.

Camille's going to be one, too. Like there's any doubt? I actually saw a Camille-of-the-Future today. Little pleated skirt, red and white pom-poms, blinding white shoes . . . but it was her voice that made me think of Camille. She talked just like Camille.

How's that, you ask?

Well, check this out. This is what the rah-rah girls were saying (and don't tell me you can't tell which one's Camille-of-the-Future):

"Ms. Sanders says someone's been, like, *living* in here!"

"Seriously? Who?"

"Like, some homeless creep! She says he's been sleeping on the gymnastics mats!"

"Oh, gross!"

"He's, like, eaten all her food! And she thinks he might, like, still be in here!"

"Really?"

"Yes! She, like, heard something crash when she unlocked the door."

"Maybe we should get out of here?"

"And leave her, like, *alone* with him? Besides, she's, like, already called the police. They'll be here any minute!"

See? You know which one's Camille, admit it. And I got this wonderful reminder of how much I missed my very best friend in the whole wide world, because the cheerleaders were having their little gossip session right by my hiding place.

The minute I'd heard people coming into the locker room, I'd cut and run, but I couldn't make it to the back door in time, and the only place I could find to hide and hold was a full-length locker.

There was barely enough room for me, let alone my backpack. I wish I'd used the backpack as a seat, but I didn't have time to think that through. I wound up folded at the knees and neck, hugging my backpack. By the time the police arrived, I'd gone from feeling like a sardine in a tin can to feeling like a pretzel of pain in a coffin.

The cops looked around awhile, then one of them started asking that Ms. Sanders lady questions.

Cop: There's a back door, correct?

Ms. Sanders: It's locked.

Cop: And the door to the gym?

Ms. Sanders: It was locked, too.

Cop: But you can exit either way without a key?

Ms. Sanders: Correct.

Cop: Is there access from here to the boys' side?

Ms. Sanders: No.

Cop: You said the phone was used?

Ms. Sanders: Yes, sir.

Cop: That might get us somewhere. [Pause.] But no
vandalism?

Ms. Sanders: Not that I've seen.

And here's where Camille-of-the-Future came skidding up to them, squealing, "Look what I found, look what I found!"

And what do you suppose she'd found?

My backup undies.

Of course she held them out like they were putrid and revolting, but all they were was tattered and damp. I'd washed them and hung them to dry over a stall divider in the bathroom.

Through the vent, I could see the cop take them and inspect the size tag, and I thought, Oh, crud!

Damp meant they were recently washed.

The size meant he was dealing with a kid.

And the type meant the kid was a girl.

I was totally busted.

Sure enough, he sighed and said, "It looks like your visitor was a girl we've been trying to track."

"A runaway?" Ms. Sanders asked him.

He nodded. "Her name's Holly. She ran away from foster care."

"How old?" Ms. Sanders asked.

"Twelve."

All the cheerleaders gasped. Then Camille-of-the-Future asked, "Is she, like, dangerous? Armed? Into drugs?"

The cop didn't answer her questions. Instead, he said, "If you see her around, just call us. Do not approach her or try to befriend her."

"Because she's, like, dangerous, armed, and into drugs?"

Again, the cop didn't answer. He just said, "Because we don't know how she'll react. Just call us."

The other cop had been combing the locker room, and one of the things he'd done was open and close a bunch of full-length lockers. But the locker room was *big,* so after a while he stopped.

When they were done talking, Ms. Sanders walked the cops out, and the instant she was gone, the cheerleaders got all gaspy and gossipy about homeless people:

"I was walking by Macy's? And I, like, accidentally *touched* one! It was so, so gross!"

"My mom bought this homeless guy a sandwich once, and when she drove past him later, she saw him feeding it to his dog!"

"Last week there was one laying on the sidewalk right around the corner from where I get my nails done! I thought he was dead!"

"I saw one passed out at that bus stop by the mall? He was lying in a puddle of pee!"

"Ooh! Gross!"

When Ms. Sanders came back, she told the rah-rah girls to get into the gym. They scurried out, and suddenly it was very, *very* quiet.

I was dying to get out of that locker. I was pinched and aching and my feet were numb, but I told myself to hold. Give it another few minutes. Make sure everyone's really gone. Hold.

And then I heard Camille-of-the-Future's voice whispering, "Holly? You can come out . . . we won't hurt you. . . ." She walked right past me. "Holly? You don't have to be afraid, we want to help you. . . ."

That made me so mad. She got grossed out just brushing up against a homeless guy, and I was supposed to believe that she wanted to help me? What a phony!

Ms. Sanders came to my rescue, calling, "Liz! Out here now!"

After that it was quiet again. And when my body just couldn't hold anymore, I worked up the latch and eased out of the locker.

At first I could barely walk. But I hobbled into the bathroom and hid in a stall until blood had found its way back into all the pinched-off places. Then I let myself out the back door, climbed a fence, and beat it out of there, checking for cops the whole time.

And now I'm back at the Greyhound station, waiting for the 6:55 bus to take me west.

I *am* going to get on board this time.

I've got a plan.

Not a foolproof plan, but it's better than the last one.

What makes me nervous is, it involves fire.

66

Same day, 7:15 p.m.

I am so stoked! And I'm wasting battery power to tell you that I am on board the Greyhound bus, heading west!

Why are you wasting battery power, you ask? Don't Greyhound buses have reading lights for their passengers?

Why, yes, they do. *If* you happen to be riding above. But I'm not riding above. I'm in the luggage hold.

The Stowaway Gypsy strikes again!

Hey, it was no easy plan to pull off, Ms. Leone. You probably don't know anything about this because I'm sure you *fly* everywhere you go, but when a bus is loading, the driver stands at the foot of the steps, taking tickets and checking luggage. He does everything. And it's hard to sneak on board *or* into the luggage compartment because he can see both and he *watches* both. Every driver I've seen has had the eyes of a hawk.

So having learned this the hard way, I knew I needed a distraction. And I knew if the distraction worked, I shouldn't get greedy. I'd been tossed off the bus before when I thought I was safe, and I didn't want to go through that again.

So what was my distraction?

Well, there was this wire-mesh trash can outside that I made sure was full of crumpled newspapers, and when the bus was in the middle of boarding, I knelt beside it and used my lighter to set it on fire.

It took a little while for it to really get going, and no one noticed it until I told the last guy in line, "Hey, look at that fire."

"Fire?" he asked, then saw it and shouted, "Fire!"

Once the commotion started and everyone was looking at the fire, I climbed into the luggage hold. It's huge in here! And since there were already lots of suitcases and boxes and stuff inside, it was easy for me to hide.

I resisted the temptation to watch them put out the fire. Hide and hold, I told myself, hide and hold. Then, after a while, more luggage came clonking in, the door clanked closed, and a few minutes later we were pulling out of the station.

We must be on the interstate now because we seem to be *flying* along. It's loud down here, but I've shoved a bunch of suitcases together and am using them as a mattress. It's actually pretty comfortable.

So that's it. In 26 hours I'll be in California.

Did you hear me?

California! Where there's sunshine and beaches and (I'm hoping) sea gypsies galore!

There are almost 20 stops between here and there, and a couple of one-hour layovers, but I picked a no-transfers route, so the same bus goes the whole way! All I have to do is stay hidden when they swap around luggage at the different stations. And since the schedule says the next stop's not for almost four hours, I'm going to nap while the napping's good.

Wish me sweet dreams, Ms. Leone!

Almost midnight

Man, I was zonked! I didn't even know the bus had come to a stop until light came flooding in when they opened the door. Lucky for me, they didn't pull out luggage right away or I'd have been busted.

Anyway, we're back on the road now and I'm wide awake, so I'm writing to tell you, Gee, thanks a lot! I ask for sweet dreams and what do I get?

A nightmare.

It went like this: I was running, running, running, through a park, through streets, over an endless bridge. . . . But halfway across the bridge the police finally nabbed me. They tossed me into a social worker's office, which at first was a normal office, but then the walls faded away, leaving jail cell bars. The social worker's desk was piled so high with papers that I couldn't see her face, but she was saying, "We're doing this because it's, like, *best* for you, Holly. You've got to learn to stop *stealing,* and, like, *lying,* and being, you know, such a social *disaster.*"

In my dream I jumped up and looked behind the mountain of papers. And no, it wasn't Camille-of-the-Future. It was the real-deal Camille!

She was wearing a blood-red suit, her hair was swirled into a bun, she had on bright red lipstick, and she was acting like she was *so* mature. And behind her, crammed between hundreds of books on a bookshelf, was a picture of you. But when I looked at the picture closer, I saw that it wasn't just a picture of you.

It was a picture of you . . . with your arm around *me.*

Stupid dream.

Tuesday, the 29th

Good thing I've got a watch and a schedule, because I've lost track of the number of stops we've made. But according to my watch and this schedule, it's high noon and we're in Arizona. According to my bladder and the temperature inside this luggage compartment, I should get out and find a bathroom and some air-conditioning.

I hope I don't fry to death down here.

2:00 p.m.

I can't believe how hot it is in here. I ransacked the luggage and found a big sports bag with a bottle of water in it. I also found a first-aid kit. I think it belongs to the bus because it was by a fire extinguisher and a whisk broom near one of the compartment doors. The good news is that the first-aid kit had an emergency ice pack in it. I'm saving it for when I can't take the heat anymore, but for now I've been drizzling the water in my hair and around my neck. It helps some, but dries so quick I can't believe it.

I also found a plastic bag in the first-aid kit, and since I was desperate, I relieved myself in that, then tied it off. Glad it's watertight. (At least it worked a lot better than the empty Gatorade bottle I used this morning.)

3:30 p.m.

I almost just bailed at the last stop. It's taking everything I've got just to breathe. But you know what? The next stop's California. A place called Barstow.

I'm hoping there are palm trees and sea gypsies and (especially) water.

I did activate the ice pack. It feels SOOOOO good.

I wish I could breathe through it.

Come on, Barstow.

5:30 p.m.

Barstow's a pit! And it must be in the middle of the bleepin' desert! The luggage door's been open for about ten minutes, but it's not helping at all. I think it's hotter out there than it is in here!

This is California?

Next stop, Riverside. Translation: city by the river.

Sounds nice.

And it's got to be better than this!

7:15 p.m.

Well, forget it. I'm staying on this bus to the end of the line. It is starting to cool off a little, and Riverside looked like a total pit, too. Not that you can tell much from the luggage hold of a bus, but I sure didn't see any palm trees or beaches or families of friendly sea gypsies.

A little before 9:00 p.m.

This is it. The end of the line. We've turned into the station, I can tell. I'm in Los Angeles.

The City of Angels!

Unbelievable!

In a few minutes they'll open the hold.

How will I get out without being arrested?

I have no idea!

(Wish me luck.)

3:00 a.m.
(That would make it, what? Wednesday the 30th?)

Checking in to say . . . Los Angeles is a nightmare! Sand? Surf? Sea gypsies? All there is, is cement! No parks, no schools, no yards . . . it goes on forever in all directions, it all looks the same, and there's no place to sleep!

Right now I'm in the scungiest McDonald's I've ever seen. It's packed with criminals. Not just losers—criminals. A real smorgasbord of drug dealers and gangsters and probably serial killers.

The ones that are freaking me out the worst are this Rastafarian dude two booths over (cloudy, bloodshot eyes, squeezing ketchup packs into his mouth and muttering something about the blood of Christ), this Cro-Magnon monster of a man who's done nothing but stare at me the whole time I've been here, and this group of guys wearing Raiders caps. (They're amped on something, and I don't think it's coffee. I'm also pretty sure one of them's got a gun.)

So why don't I just leave?

Because outside's worse! It's like some weird horror movie where the ghouls come out at night and walk the streets looking for souls to capture and kill.

And I *was* being followed, too. Some creepy guys in an old clunker car. Every street I turned down, there they were again. I managed to ditch them for a little while, but they found me again. It freaked me out bad, so I ducked in here.

4:30 a.m., still the night of the living dead

You should see the bathroom. It's a disaster! Everything's plugged. Overflowing. Written on. It's wall-to-wall feces and graffiti.

Like you needed to know that?

Well, go fluff your potpourri, Ms. Leone. This ain't Neverland.

But speaking of which, I wonder where Disneyland is. I know it's around here somewhere. I wonder if it's like an oasis in the middle of a cement-and-graffiti desert.

I don't care about the rides. I just want some trees and grass. A place to sleep. Wouldn't that be something? Being a Disneyland gypsy? There are probably all sorts of great places to hide. Maybe I'd sneak into the Pirates of the Caribbean—I've heard that's an awesome ride, with real water and ships and cute little pirate doggies. . . .

Back to the real world:

I've changed seats three times. The Cro-Magnon creep has, too. And the only reason I'm writing in this is because I can't sit here staring at the wall until sunrise, and I sure don't want to make eye contact with any of the losers in this joint. I'm just trying to look like I've got a *purpose* for being here, that's all.

In a bizarre way this dive reminds me of my first day in your classroom. I could tell you'd told the class about my "unfortunate background." Don't deny it. Knowing you, you told them to be "sensitive

73

to the situation" and used all the concerned-citizen buzzwords. They're words I've heard for years, and guess what, Ms. Leone. They don't do squat to help the situation.

You want to know what *would* have helped?

If you'd just kept your mouth shut.

Or maybe if you'd said, "Class, we have a new student joining us tomorrow. Her name's Holly Janquell, and the two things she loves most in the world are reading and dogs. So if you have a favorite book you'd like to tell her about, or if you have pictures of your dog you'd like to bring in, it might help to make her feel welcome. And remember, it's not easy transferring to a new school this late in the year, so just pretend it's *you* and treat her like you'd want to be treated."

They *still* would have snubbed me when you weren't looking, but it would have been better than having them treat me like a freak.

I'm not trying to rag on you, I actually think it's funny that being here reminds me of school: all these people looking at me like I don't belong. Giving me suspicious looks. Or ignoring me but then checking me over, head to toe, when they think I'm not looking. It's just like school! They don't understand why I'm here, they don't *like* that I'm here, and even though they've got their own "issues" to deal with, in the back of their minds they're going, Somebody get *rid* of her.

Actually, I wish you could be here because you know what? You'd look around and go, Good God, Holly! *This* is what school felt like for you? I think something might go *click* inside your head. (Don't *even* tell me you understand. You *think* you do, but I promise you, you don't.)

Oh, look! It's getting light out!

And there are people waiting to cross at the intersection. *Real* people.

Time to move on!

The night of the living dead is finally OVER.

July 4th

I about had a heart attack when somebody lit off firecrackers. I thought they were gunshots again. What sort of moron lights off firecrackers under a bridge?

I'd lost track, but now I know it's Independence Day.

Excuse me if I don't celebrate.

In case you're wondering, I wasn't going to write you again until I could say, Eureka! I've found surf! Sand! A friendly family of sea gypsies! Life is good! Then I'd cap it all off with a happy little poem and you wouldn't think I was stupid or crazy or completely naïve.

Tonight *I'm* the one thinking I'm stupid and crazy and completely naïve.

I can't keep living like this.

I can't even talk about it.

This is no City of Angels.

It's Hell on Earth.

Almost midnight

I thought a lot about the Underground Railroad tonight. Probably because it's Independence Day, which makes you think about freedom.

You probably figured I wasn't paying attention when you told us about the Underground Railroad, but I was. I liked the whole story, the whole idea of all these different people making secret rooms and hideouts to help slaves escape to the North. I liked the secret message in the "Drinking Gourd" song that explained how to use the Big Dipper to get to the next safe house. I liked how the escaping slaves learned to keep slave-hunter dogs from tracking them by rubbing their feet with onions. I liked the story about that guy, Fairchild, who put on different disguises to help the slaves and snuck twenty-eight of them to freedom at once by putting them in a hearse and pretending it was a funeral.

But what I've been thinking about most is the way your voice quivered when you read what Harriet Tubman had said. (That was her name, right? The slave who was about to be sold and thought she'd never see her family again?) It's like her words are stuck in my head, speaking through you to me:

"There was one of two things I had a right to: liberty or death. If I could not have one, I would take the other, for no man should take me alive. I should fight for my liberty as long as my strength lasted."

The way your voice quivered . . . it's like you really understood what she'd been through. And I would never have actually *told* you this, but when you read that to the class, it made my eyes sting.

So why am I bringing this up?

Because I'm hoping you'll understand this, too:

I'd give anything to find an underground railroad for runaways. I'd give anything to know some people I could trust. I'd give anything to not be so scared and hungry and afraid of being caught.

I'd give anything to be free.

The next day

I've decided this is all your fault. I've run away before, you know, but I never stowed away or jumped trains or broke into buildings.

I just ran away and got caught.

But I think all that stuff you told us about the Underground Railroad got lodged in my subconscious, and somewhere inside it gave me the strength or courage or *insanity* to really get away.

So see?

This is all your fault.

July something

I haven't written in a long time because I didn't want to actually say how miserable I've been. I keep thinking that I'll get *out* of here and *then* tell you about the better place I've found. I guess it's okay to admit you're miserable if you've got some plan to change things. But just saying, "I'm so miserable!" seems helpless and hopeless and *whiny.* Like something Camille would do.

I have totally lost track of what day it is. I have no money because my second day here I got tackled by some hoodlums and they ripped me off. Every cent. At the time I was so scared that they were going to hurt me bad or kill me that I was glad they only took my money. But now I'm stuck in a vicious cycle of wasting the day finding food, eating, sleeping, then waking up hungry again.

I can't seem to find my way out of this place. Normally I've got a pretty good sense of direction. I just use the sun and the time of day, and I get pretty close. But around here the sun doesn't really show itself. The sky is foggy sometimes, smoggy most times, and the buildings are tall and block the sky. I walk and walk and walk, and I *think* I know where I'm going, but it's so loud and dusty and intense here, and somehow I wind up getting turned around.

Los Angeles is *huge*. It has places where freeways crisscross above each other four or five levels high. Places where there is nothing but roads going every which way for as far as the eye can see. And you can't tell where a road will lead because they're not laid out in a grid. They curve. Some loop clear around. I feel so disoriented. Like I've been swallowed up by a dirty, heartless, cement-and-asphalt monster that has freeways for arteries and cars for blood.

I also haven't been able to do any of the survival things I'm used to being able to do. I have yet to see a 7-Eleven, and all the gas stations have bulletproof-looking kiosks where people pay for gas. No store, no posted maps . . . some of them don't even have people working in them. They're totally automated.

I did hear about a place called The People's Church. It supposedly gives food and shelter to the needy, but I haven't been able to find it.

Why don't I just ask someone?

Well, when you're twelve and you're homeless . . . CRUD! I'm NOT homeless. I'm a gypsy! A GYPSY! I am . . .

> *G*utsy and fearless!
> *Y*esterday's jailbreak!
> *P*lucky like a pirate!
> *S*hrewd and speedy!
> *Y*earning to be free!

> I am a *GYPSY!*

And when you're a twelve-year-old gypsy, you can't ask, "Excuse me, sir. I heard there's a church that offers shelter and food to those in need . . . can you tell me where it is?" They'll get all nosy or call the police and pretty soon you're back in the system, locked in a closet.

I *have* asked a few people, "Excuse me, is there a church nearby?" but they've all said the same thing as they've hurried away: "A *church*? Around *here*?"

Nobody stands still in this city. Not even the homeless. Everybody seems scared of everybody else. The shops all have bars on their windows and security guards posted at the doors. I haven't been able to lift any food because the few markets I've seen are all on high alert.

So I might as well just tell you: I've been eating from trash cans.

And nothing's been from above the rim.

Go ahead and be revolted, see if I care. I can't fight for my liberty if I'm starving (which I am). I need strength if I'm going to last (which, if Harriet Tubman did, so can I). And if that means eating from the trash, that's what I'm going to do.

It's called survival.

Wednesday, July 28th (if the newspaper I saw is today's, anyway . . .)

Remember I told you how I lose my sense of direction in this place? Well, today I thought I was walking west, but I was actually walking east. And instead of finding a church with a shelter, I found the Los Angeles River.

Ah, you say. Refreshing water! Trees! Perhaps fish to catch for supper?

79

Guess again.

Even the *river* here is cement. I'm not kidding. The sign says LOS ANGELES RIVER but it's a giant canal of cement with no water in it. The "banks" are cement, too, decorated in huge areas with graffiti. All you can see in any direction are power lines and train tracks and cement, cement, cement.

I decided to walk "downstream." It was dusk and I was really hungry, but I saw no chance of finding any food around the "river," so I just wanted to find a safe place to sleep before it got too dark. A place where I could see people coming before they could see me. A place where my back was protected and my body was sheltered.

I was starting to think that the river was a horrible choice because there were train tracks on either side of it and, beyond them, an endless, barren wasteland of industrial buildings. But then I spotted an overpass, and as I got closer, I saw a shopping cart. It was upright, at the foot of the bank near the overpass.

I ducked through a large break in the chain-link fence and walked along the cement riverbank toward the cement overpass that crossed above the cement river. I was quiet and careful, and when I got closer, I smelled cigarettes.

Under the overpass was a small camp of homeless: three women (two of them with little babies) plus about five men. I spied on them from behind the arch of the overpass for a few minutes, then stepped forward with my hands up, saying, "Hello? Is it okay if I come in?"

There was a lot of quick chattering in Spanish, and finally one of the women said, "You are lost?"

I nodded, then shook my head, then shrugged.

The woman laughed.

"Tired?" she asked.

I nodded.

"Hungry?"

I nodded before I could stop and think that they might chase me away if they thought I wanted their food.

She smiled kindly and patted the ground beside her.

I stepped into the shade of the overpass, thinking that this had gone way too easy. Maybe they were all going to surround me and pounce. Maybe . . .

But the woman smiled again and said, "Is okay. Come." She patted the ground some more, then chattered in Spanish at the men, waving them off.

The men backed away, so I took a few more steps toward her and said, "Thank you."

"De nada," she said. Then she rummaged around a canvas sack and pulled out a can of hash. "You like?"

I almost broke into tears. She was being so nice. And I was so, so hungry.

"For you," she said, pushing it on me.

I sat down and pried open the lid. My hands were shaking. My legs were shaking. My mouth was watering like a dog's.

"No eat too fast," she said, then handed me two sort of dried-out corn tortillas. "Use." She tore off a piece and pinched it over some hash. "See?"

So that's how I ate. A little tortilla wrapped around a bit of hash. I ate every morsel. Every crumb. Every *molecule.* And when I was done, she smiled and said, "Better?"

I nodded. And I tried not to, but my chin quivered and my eyes stung as I told her, "Thank you."

So I've been thinking that this place by the cement river is like my first safe house. And it may sound stupid and naïve to you, but thinking that way fills me with hope. And stupid and naïve or not, without hope I've got nothing.

3:20 a.m.

steel screeches on

the track

reaches on

the night spans gray

and lights

burn my eyes

as night

reaches on,

endlessly on

The next day

I had a miserable night last night, but right now I am in the ab-
solute best mood. You are not going to believe where I am!

I happened to find this place while I was searching again for The
People's Church. (My friends from last night tried to give me directions to the church, but I don't think I understood right.)

But forget that. Right now I'm inside the coolest building I have

83

ever seen. It's big, with tall ceilings and echoing halls, and it's full of wood and (of course) cement. But this is good cement!

So where am I?

Here's a big hint: I haven't told you the *main* thing they have here.

Big hint #2: You would love it here!

Give up?

I'm in the *library.*

This is nothing like that podunk hardly-ever-open Aaronville library (or any other library I've been in, for that matter). This place is a *museum* of books. Floor after floor of books! I wandered around for hours and am now in the teen section. It's unbelievable here: cushy couches and coffee tables and magazines . . . it's more like a *lounge* than a library.

I've picked out a few books, too. There's one about escaping from Alcatraz. (You've heard of Alcatraz, right? That old prison on an island? I never knew this, but it's in California. I'm not sure if the book is fact or fiction, but it sounds great!)

Another book I picked out is about an evil boy who terrorizes people during the day, but at night he turns into a benevolent ghost and goes around helping people. What is he, evil or good? I guess I have to read it to find out.

But the one I'm going to read first is about this girl who gets stranded on a desert island with her dog. What a perfect life! You should see the cover—the girl looks sort of lame, but the dog is so happy-looking! (What I would give to be stranded on a desert island with a dog that cute. . . .)

I could probably sneak the books out of the library, but why would

I? It's cool and comfortable in here, and there's no traffic noise. Plus, the bathrooms are nice, and everybody's minding their own business.

Too bad the library closes at eight.

Too bad they don't have free food.

But forget about that. I'll deal with sleep and hunger later. Right now I'm going to sit in this cushy chair and read!

3:45 p.m.

Guess what! I found a room with a refrigerator and scored big-time! Two sandwiches, a couple of yogurts, a can of almonds, and some beef jerky. I stashed them in my jacket quick, then went into a bathroom stall, scarfed some of it down, and put the rest in my backpack.

I love this place!

7:45 p.m.

The library's closing in 15 minutes. And all of a sudden I'm really, really tired. I shouldn't have spent the whole day reading. I should have found that church. Or I should have taken a nap in here.

Maybe I'll hide behind the bookshelves and wait for the place to close down. It would be so nice to sleep on a couch. . . .

But what if they have night security? What if I get caught? They'll know I'm ~~homele~~ a *gypsy.* They'll turn me in.

Crud.

10:30 p.m.

There *are* guards roaming around. Two, I think. They cruised through the teen section but haven't come back for a while. I can't see any cameras mounted on the walls, scanning the room for tired gyp-sies, so I'm hoping I'm safe for the night.

I'm going to forget the couch (even though it's calling my name really LOUD). It's in the wide-open middle of this room, and they'd see me for sure if they came through again. I thought about snagging two of the couch cushions and bringing them back here, but then I can't pretend to have fallen asleep during business hours if I get caught. (That's what I'm planning to say if they find me. You know, "Oh no! I can't believe it! I've got to get home. My mother is going to be SO worried!")

Better safe and uncomfortable than comfy and caught.

The next day, 8:45 a.m.

Close call! I was on my way to the bathroom, because my bladder could not make it to opening time to get relieved, when this lady came into the teen section with a cart of books. I held really, really still, and she was so busy rolling the cart around, putting books on the shelves, that she didn't notice me. The minute she went around a stack, I beat it into the bathroom.

So now I'm in a stall, killing time before the library opens. I hope there's some librarian's lavatory that they use instead of this one. One look at my shoes under the divider and they'll know I don't work here. Then they'll bust me and find a yogurt container and cellophane and figure out that I just had their lunch for breakfast.

Same next day, 10:45 a.m.

Back in my teen-section chair, comfy and fairly safe. I did get The Look from a librarian. At least I *think* she's a librarian. She asked me, "Weren't you here yesterday?"

"Yes, ma'am," I said with a smile. "I love the library." Then I added, "My mom's a lawyer, and I beg her to take me here whenever she has to do research. I love books, and getting to spend whole days at the library is just the best!"

So okay, I laid it on pretty thick. But she smiled and nodded, and I think the bit about my mom being a lawyer was a stroke of genius, don't you? Who wants to mess with a girl whose mother is a lawyer?

Just call me the Genius Gypsy!

Ha ha!

But the truth is, this genius gypsy is starting to wonder what in the world she's doing. I can't stay in a library in the middle of a cement city. I don't want to be a cement-city gypsy. I'm a *sea* gypsy. A genius gypsy of the sea, that's me!

3:15 p.m.

I finished that book about the girl and the dog. The dog saved her life about twenty times, then in the end he died. Stupid book. I buried it in the bathroom trash bin, which is where a book like that belongs.

The story about escaping Alcatraz was a lot better. I like escaping books. I can relate.

So I've started on the one with the ghost boy and so far it's really good, but I'm distracted because I'm worrying about tonight. I've gotten The Look about ten times in the past hour, and I know the clock is ticking. I tried to wash up in the bathroom, but it's not even close to the same thing as a shower. And no matter how polite I act, my clothes are filthy and I know I look awful.

I guess it's time for me to find that church.

I wish I could get a library card. I'd really like to finish this book.

I guess I'll have to steal it.

8:00 p.m.

When I realized my little vacation at the library was coming to an end, I started getting really stressed out. I didn't want to go back outside! I started thinking about how long it takes to go *anywhere* in this city. How depressed and disoriented and hungry I've been living here. But then I got the brilliant idea that the library might have *maps,* and it does! Tons of them!

And guess what?

I'm only about 15 miles from the ocean! I could walk that in a day! (Or two.) And I can go south *or* west. The coastline curves around, so either way I'll wind up at the Pacific Ocean!

I also found out that I'm about 12 miles from Beverly Hills and only 8 miles from Hollywood. But who cares about them, right? I want to see the sea! I want to jump right in and take a giant salt bath! I want to swim with the dolphins and make a lean-to out of palm fronds and watch birds swoop through the sky!

I was so excited to know my way out of this cement trap that I almost just started walking. But I was also hungry and needed a shower

88

and clean clothes. So first I looked up the *address* of The People's Church in the phone book (which they also have tons of at the library.)

And no wonder I couldn't find it! It doesn't look anything *like* a church. No pointy roof or stained-glass windows. No crosses or statues of Jesus or Mary or angels. Just a little sign posted on a basement door that says THE PEOPLE'S CHURCH.

It's an actual underground church!

I told the pastor, "My mom said to meet her here because—" But before I could even finish building up my lie, he waved me in. "Come! Come in! The House of the Lord welcomes all. I'm Reverend Raynaldo, this is Shanana, and we're here to help you any way we can."

I don't know what you think about God, Ms. Leone, but the days I'm not busy hating him, I think he doesn't exist. Or if he does, he's just the devil with a white cloak on. Like Ghost Boy. Which is he? Good or evil? (I may never know, because I got busted trying to lift the book.)

But there is no doubt in Reverend Raynaldo's and Shanana's minds about God. They are believers, and you know what? It's nice to be around them. I've taken a shower, gotten clean clothes, eaten a TON of baked spaghetti, and I've got my own mat, pillow, and blanket over here in the corner. And they haven't asked me once, "So . . . when did you say your mother was coming?"

If it wasn't for the winos and druggies and schizos (who also have mats, pillows, and blankets), I might actually feel comfortable here.

Sunday night, August 1st

Summer is going by fast and I haven't even seen the ocean, let alone frolicked with dolphins. I wasted yesterday sleeping. I swear, except for stuffing my face during breakfast, lunch, and dinner, I slept the whole day away. And I wasn't wide awake at night, in case you're wondering. I slept the whole night away, too.

It felt so good.

And still no questions about my mother.

Shanana made me go to church this morning. "Time to give thanks," she told me. "Time to let Him hear your gratitude."

"I'm grateful to you, anyway," I muttered.

"I'm just the messenger," she said with a smile. "Tell Him."

So I went into the "chapel" (a cramped room with a very low ceiling and dilapidated folding chairs), and I listened to Reverend Raynaldo sermonize about the bounty of blessings the Lord has laid on the table for our feasting, and how the Light is the way for God's lost flock to find its way Home.

I also listened to a lot of snorting and hacking and snoring from the homeless gallery. Plus, this one really spaced-out guy kept shouting stuff like "I am the One, the Way, and the Light! Follow me! To the desert! I have camels!"

I've met a lot of guys who think they're Jesus. Maybe it happens when your beard gets long and scraggly and you start looking like a guy who's walked across the desert in sandals. But this particular Jesus had the worst slur and most bloodshot eyes of any of the "prophets" I've ever seen. Shanana finally got him to leave, but she was amazingly

90

nice about it. I'd have grabbed him by the ear and tossed him out on his rear.

I was surprised to see so many children at the service. I don't know why any mom would bring her kids to this church, but a lot of them did. Maybe it's the bounty of donuts and orange drink and coffee that the reverend and Shanana put out. After the sermon, everyone pigged out, tanked up, and took off.

Talking about God made me remember the Blue Lady. Have you ever heard of her? (What am I saying. Of course you haven't.) The Blue Lady's a secret among street kids, and the sad thing is, I used to believe in her. I really, truly used to believe in her. I wanted so badly for her to be real.

I'm not supposed to tell you about the Blue Lady, but I'm going to. Ready?

Here's how the legend goes:

Years ago now, God fled his beautiful marble palace in Heaven to escape a treacherous attack of Hell's most powerful demons. The demons, with their scaly skins and eyes of dripping blood, smashed the palace until it was nothing but dust. The angels in Heaven were stunned. Where had God gone? Why didn't He return? How could they defend Earth from the demons of the underworld without Him?

Time passed. God did not return. And demons found doorways into our world through abandoned refrigerators, mirrors, and limousines with blackened windows. Once on Earth, demons thrived on dark human emotions like fear and hate and jealousy.

The most feared demon of all (feared even by Satan) is a woman whose black dress billows backward, even on the stillest of nights. Blood drips from her ghoulish empty eye sockets as she screeches and howls at lesser demons to obey her. She is called the Crying Woman, and she is the one who led the attack on Heaven. And now that she is on Earth, she grows in power and strength by feeding on the terror of children.

There is one angel who can fight off the Crying Woman. She is beautiful, with long, flowing hair and glowing blue skin, and she lives in the ocean. She wants to save children from the Crying Woman but can only do so if they call out her secret name: the Blue Lady.

When the Blue Lady hears a child cry to her for help, she quickly gathers an angel army to protect the child from danger. Flying bullets, demons disguised as men, fever, or famine . . . if you call out to the Blue Lady, she will find a way to rescue you. You will hear her gentle voice whispering in your ear, "Hold on. You will be safe. Hold on." She is good and kind and strong, and if you hold on, you will be safe. So hold on.

I used to love that story. I first heard it when I was nine. An older boy, maybe eleven or twelve, whispered the story to a group of us in the children's corner at a shelter. "No adults can know about her," he told us. "Adults don't believe. Adults make fun. But it's true. I swear on my father's grave, it's true."

Some of the other kids nodded and whispered, "I've seen her." "She saved me." "She's like an angel ghost, only blue."

I heard the story of the Blue Lady many times, from all sorts of kids. And then at one shelter, I was the oldest, so it was my job to tell it. I loved seeing the younger kids' eyes grow wide with awe as they heard the story for the first time.

I also loved the power of the Blue Lady. The strength she gave us on the inside. Like we *could* hold on because she and her army of angels were on a mission to protect us from evil, and somehow, some way, we would win.

I used to cry out to the Blue Lady when things got really bad. I used to think I heard her voice whisper, "Hold on, Holly. You will be safe. Hold on."

But then I found my mother.

Dead.

And now I know:

There is no Blue Lady.

There's only wishful dreaming.

4:45 p.m. I think it's Thursday. I've lost track again.

I should know better than to walk along main streets. Cops use main streets. But when I left The People's Church, I wanted to get out of Cement City and to the ocean as fast as I could. And I didn't want to get turned around again. So I headed west the way I'd memorized from the map at the library: Follow Wilshire Blvd. (By the way, just so you don't think I'm stupid, I decided to go west instead of south because on the map there were more green spaces along Wilshire, and following the Los Angeles River south to the ocean seemed very depressing. Plus, I started thinking that with the way they pour cement around here, the Cement River probably leads to Concrete Beach.)

I almost asked Shanana about the beaches and which one she

thought was the best (because according to the map, there are miles and miles of them), but I really didn't want her or the reverend to know where I was planning to go. And I'm glad I didn't because Shanana started bringing up my mother.

"Sweet child," she said, "I think we should get you some help. That mama of yours is just not showing up."

"Oh, she's coming," I told her, like I really believed it. "We've done this before. You don't *mind* me staying here, do you?"

"No, of course not! I'm just hopin' everything's okay."

"Everything's fine," I said. "And you've been really, really nice."

So I acted like I was planning to stay on longer, but the first chance I got, I stashed away a ton of food and took off.

I found Wilshire Blvd. and I tried to pace myself as I walked. Not too fast or you look suspicious. Not too slow or you look unsure. But it's been really, really hot here, and it's hard to move at a steady pace. According to a big billboard temperature sign that I saw, it was 101 degrees yesterday. Actually, I'm sure it was even hotter than that. You know how they factor in wind chill when it's really cold, which makes the temperature even *colder*? ("Last night's low was thirty-one degrees, but with wind chill, that figure dropped to nineteen.") Well, around here there's the opposite of wind chill. There's asphalt heat. I swear heat radiates off the street and jacks the temperature up another ten degrees. And all the air conditioners that are cranked up to cool off the inside of buildings pump hot air *outside*. So up in the sky where they've got that temperature sign it may be 101 degrees, but down here on the street with the fire-breathing air conditioners and asphalt, it's more like 120 degrees.

WHERE'S THE OCEAN???????

Too late to find that today, so let me finish telling you about the cops:

The same cop saw me, two days in a row. I recognized her, because how many cops do you see with wraparound shades and bleached cornrows? And she recognized me, because how many twelve-year-olds with green corduroy pants (that's all they had at The People's Church that fit me) and an overstuffed backpack do you see hiking down the same street, *miles* from where you'd spotted them the day before?

But instead of doing something really constructive like offering me a lift to the ocean so I could jump in and COOL OFF, she pulled over and called, "Excuse me?"

I didn't pay one bit of attention to her. I just kept walking.

"Excuse me?" she said again, and this time she came onto the sidewalk.

I smiled at her and kept walking.

"Stop!" she commanded. "I'm talking to you!"

I turned and did something my mom used to do. I asked her, *"Pardonnez-moi?"* like I didn't understand a word she was saying.

She frowned at me and said, "You some two-pint tourist?"

I only know about three French words, but that's all my mom knew, either, so I did what she used to do: I made up whole sentences of phony French, shoving them through my nose as I spoke.

"Stop!" the cop snapped. "You don't understand English?"

"Oui! Oui!" I said, then spoke a bunch more phony French. And, in an effort to get away from her, I channeled my phony mother, *Louise,* as I curtsied and said, *"Au revoir!"*

95

It worked. The cop threw her hands in the air, made some grumbling sounds, and got back in her cruiser.

Inside, I felt really good. Like both my mother and Louise were watching over me, helping me.

Crud. There I go again. I hate getting all weepy about my mom. Why isn't she here with me? Why did she have to go and OD? I hate Eddie for getting her hooked, you hear me? I hate him, hate him, hate him! If he wasn't dead already, I swear I'd kill him.

Lousy good-for-nothing creep.

But I really don't want to talk about him or her. I was working up to telling you about this dog named Knobs, so that's what I'm going to do.

After I ditched that cop, I got off the main drag quick, thinking it would be smarter to follow a parallel, less patrolled road. That's when I spotted Knobs coming out from between some buildings. All of a sudden it seemed like ages since I'd seen a dog. You know, *petted* a dog. So I started walking quicker and called, "Here, boy!" (I didn't know his name yet.) I whistled and said it again. "Here, boy!"

He glanced over his shoulder as he pranced along the sidewalk in front of me. So I said, "Hey, wait up, fella! What's your name?"

He walked a little faster but kept looking over his shoulder. Not like he was afraid of me. More like he had someplace to get to and sort of wanted me to come along.

So I followed him. Up the street. Over. Up another street. Over. Up another street. Zigzag, zigzag we went until we got to a park. It was small and scroungy, with a lot of dead grass and scrawny trees and graffiti. But Knobs waited by the water fountain, tail wagging, obviously wanting me to push the button so he could jump up and get a drink.

See? Dogs are smart.

After we'd both lapped up about a gallon of water, I read his tag and started calling him his name and just ruffled and hugged and let him happy me up. He was so panty and waggy and sweet. I tossed a stick for him some, I shared my food with him. (I gave him the stuff that was getting pretty borderline from baking in my backpack in the sun.) Then I gave him another drink from the fountain and got a drink myself, but when I turned back around, he was gone.

You probably already figured this out, but I was so busy following Knobs that I got totally lost. And when I started walking again, I *thought* I knew which way was west, but my west turned out to be north. And do you know where I am now?

Beverly Hills!

This area is like the *opposite* of where I've just come from, and something about that is so, so weird. How did it go from concrete, barbed-wire fences, graffiti walls, and scroungy, scraggly brown grass to *this* in just a few blocks? There are palm trees. Tall, graceful palm trees. Whole streets are lined with them. And you should see the lawns these people have! They're like lush oceans of grass. And the temperature is a good twenty degrees cooler here, too. I'm not exaggerating.

So, are these movie-star homes?

I have no idea.

But I can tell you this: There's one person who spent last night in Beverly Hills who is definitely not a movie star.

She's a sea gypsy!

Ha ha!

And you should see the stuff these people throw away. The food in their trash bins could feed an army! I had some kind of cheesy scones, a baked potato (with plenty of butter and sour cream still on it!), and the rind of a roast beef for dinner.

Yum!

Plus, I found a great hideaway behind some shrubs in an amazing backyard. You wouldn't believe this backyard. It has actual rolling hills for a lawn, plus a tennis court, a swimming pool, and the most beautiful purple-flowered trees I've ever seen.

It's nice here.

Real nice.

Same backyard, a couple days later

There's a girl who gets a tennis lesson every day at 10:00. I may not know her, but I still hate her.

Picture this: white tennis skirt and tank top, spotless shoes, a white sun visor, sweat bands around both wrists, and sleek hair pulled back into a perfect braid.

Oh, you're thinking, poor you. You're jealous.

Okay, I admit it. I am a little. But that's not why I hate her. I hate her because she's snotty and whiny. I hate her because she's got opportunity but no drive. That little diva doesn't even *try*. You should hear her talk back to the instructor: "You hit it too hard!" "I'm not doing backhand today!" "My ankle hurts!" "You *told* me to do it like that. Make up your mind!"

I'd like to slap her silly! If I could switch places with her, I'd work my heart out. I'd listen. I'd sweat. I'd *try*.

Switching places with her would be funny, actually. Her living in the shrubs, me in the house? Sort of like *The Prince and the Pauper,* only it'd be *The Princess and the Gypsy.* I'd enjoy the good life, she'd learn to eat out of garbage cans. I'd become a tennis pro, she'd learn to regret not appreciating what she had.

Nice thought, but it's not going to happen. Reality is, I'm stuck in the bushes. Reality is, I spend my whole day thinking about food and shelter and about how not to get caught. Reality is, I may have survived two months as a gypsy, but I've got six more years to go before I can get a job and rent an apartment and buy real food.

Six more *years.*

Am I really going to keep doing this for six more years?

Okay. The princess's lesson is over now, and I'm going to say this because I'm hoping it'll help me sort things out:

I don't want to watch other people play tennis for six years. I can barely stand doing it for three days.

I don't want to eat other people's garbage for six *years.*

I don't want to run and hide and lie and steal for six *years.*

I don't want to feel this all-alone.

I don't want to be this *bored.*

That's it, right there. That's the one that's bugging me the most. I'm bored. If my stomach's not aching and I'm not tired or scared or on the run, I'm sitting around with nothing to do. Why do you think I write in this thing? And six more *years* of this? I don't know if I can

99

take that. And then what? When I'm finally eighteen, how am I going to get a job? I haven't even finished elementary school! Nobody's going to hire me. So where's that leave me? On the streets? Sleeping in bushes, eating out of trash cans?

Well, at least I'd be able to get into shelters, but I don't *want* to live in shelters. I want a home! I want a dog! I want someplace where I belong.

And you know what? While I'm actually saying all this, I'm going to tell you something else. When I grow up, you know what I'd really, really love to be?

A dog doctor.

Forget cats, forget horses, I'd be a veterinarian who specialized in dogs. I'd be the best, too. People would come from miles around because they'd heard about Dr. Holly Janquell's special way with dogs.

I can't believe I actually told you that.

I'm a homeless girl, hiding in the bushes, dreaming about becoming a vet.

How pathetic is that?

Two (?) days later

This is a weird neighborhood. Everyone's got a full-blown park for a backyard (and some for a front yard), but you rarely see anyone around. Cars zoom by on the main road, but the "estates" are dead. Where are all the people? Why aren't they using their pools? Why aren't they out playing golf on their back lawns? Are they too old? Are they on location somewhere making movies? Why have a million-dollar estate if you're not going to use it?

I don't get it.

I don't get it at all.

Who knows what day it is . . .

I finally got caught by the gardener. He didn't *catch* me catch me, he just saw me and chased me off. Better him than that bratty girl, that's for sure. She'd have screeched for the police. He just chattered in Spanish and came after me with his leaf blower.

I think I was just waiting to get caught. I was there way too long. Beverly Hills was not my destination, and really, I was wasting my time hanging out in the safety of that backyard. I guess I just got comfortable there. It may not have been the beach, but compared to the cement jungle? It was paradise.

Hmm. Maybe that's what happens if you get comfortable someplace. Maybe you need some motivation to move on. Actually, now that I think about it, maybe it's not just being comfortable. Maybe it's being *used to.* A place can be very *un*comfortable, but if you're used to it, it gives you a strange sense of comfort. Did that make any sense? For example, why do people stay in places or jobs or relationships that they hate? Why don't they just leave?

Because they're used to it, that's why.

Wait a minute, I can hear you saying. Not everyone's willing to chuck the little they've got and eat out of trash cans.

If it means winding up someplace better than where they were, why not?

Oh, so you don't think I'm better off than I was?

That's because you don't get it, Ms. Leone. You don't get it and

101

you probably never will. Here's the truth: I would WAY rather be hungry and tired and scared on the streets of L.A. than put up with the "comfort and safety" of the Benders' house.

I wouldn't go back there for all the silk sheets in China.

And if you don't think I'm better off than I was, you should see this day! It is drop-dead gorgeous. It's *hot,* but I'm sitting on a park bench in the shade, and there's lots of grass and a nice, cool breeze, and it doesn't *feel* hot.

Ha! I just got a little mental picture of you: You're *in*doors with the air-conditioning cranked way up because it's 100 degrees and 98% humidity outside and the mosquitoes are swarming and the bugs are atrocious. Am I right? Summers there are awful! *Winters* there are awful. See? Why do you stay? You ought to run away! Hop a train! Stow away on a bus!

What am I saying? You could just buy yourself a ticket.

It would be interesting to talk to you if you did it the other way, though.

We could compare scars and bruises.

It might be fun.

3:10 p.m.

I've been sitting here, thinking *again* about how I talk to you like you're really there. Not out loud like some crazy street person, don't be stupid. I mean in this thing. I wouldn't say two words to you in school, but now I chat away about everything, even the weather.

That's weird enough right there, but what's even weirder is that it really feels like I'm talking to someone.

It really feels like I'm talking to *you*.

Why is that?

And why do I keep doing it when I know I'm never going to see you again?

4:30 p.m.

I just found out that it's the 18th of August. Unbelievable! How can it be the 18th of August?

Time is a weird thing. In some ways it feels like I *just* left The People's Church.

In some ways it feels like forever ago.

There's that ebb and flow in my mind about other things, too. Where it feels really close, then way far away. The Benders, the train, the bus, Louise, the library, my mother . . . waves of memories that wash in, then wash out. Close, then far.

Fear's like that, too.

Still August 18ᵗʰ, 10 p.m.

I didn't want to admit it before, but the wave of fear was crashing, and crashing hard. Everywhere I go, I try to stay in the background. And that great warm-and-breezy park I told you about was the perfect place to spend the day, and maybe the night. But there was this man there. He had thin hair, combed back. He was a little paunchy but not bad, and was of medium height. Just your average middle-aged Joe.

He wasn't homeless. He was wearing businessman pants and shoes, sunglasses, and was clean-shaven. At first I thought he was just enjoying an afternoon in the park, but then I realized that he wasn't really reading his newspaper.

He was watching the playground.

I kept a sly eye on him. He gave me the creeps like I haven't felt in ages. And I made up my mind that nothing was going to stop me from tackling him if he tried to snatch a kid. I'd go down in a splat of gypsy glory if I had to, but there was no way I was going to let him touch a kid.

I was keyed up for over an hour because of this guy. He brought back all these feelings of being little and vulnerable and scared and confused, of gaping wounds in the heart that no one can see.

But then he put down his newspaper and left.

You know how the D.A.R.E. people came to school and told us that drugs burn holes in your brain or make you paranoid or have flashbacks or, you know, do permanent damage to your head? Well, after that guy left, I started worrying that maybe my experiences have been like drugs to my brain. Maybe they're making me have flashbacks or paranoia, or they've permanently branded my brain with suspicion. The guy was probably just enjoying the beautiful afternoon, remembering the carefree joy of his youth by watching kids frolic in the park.

After a few minutes I went over and got his newspaper (which is how I found out what day it is). I actually sat on his bench for a while, but it felt kind of creepy. Like he was still there.

So I went to *another* bench, where I wrote in this and read the paper.

But I still had that creepy feeling, so I left the paper behind and moved again, and that's when I noticed someone lurking in the shadows of the trees behind the bench where I'd been sitting. It was the same man, and he wasn't watching the kids on the playground.

He was watching me.

I took off quick. And I thought I'd ditched him, only when I came out of the Grab and Go mini-market (where I'd done just that, and was all keyed up about it because all I'd gotten was a protein bar and it hadn't exactly been *easy*), I saw him in a car in the parking lot.

I almost pointed and shouted, That guy is stalking me! You hear me? If I wind up dead, it'll be because of that guy right there! But I didn't do that because people would have taken one look at me and thought, Deranged homeless girl. Probably on drugs.

So what would you have done, Ms. Leone? Called the cops?

Well, that's not exactly an option for me, is it. So what I did was go behind his car to write down his license plate in *this* thing. That way if he did snatch me and murder me, there'd be a trail of evidence.

But guess what?

He didn't *have* a license plate.

Isn't that great? Cops will interrogate me for walking down the sidewalk, but they let a guy like him prowl around without a license plate. Maybe he has one that he props in the back window when he's not in pervert mode, but there was no plate when I looked. So I went up to the driver's-side window and shouted, "I'm telling the cops about you, buddy. You are one sick sucker and you'd better leave me alone!" Then I moved away quick, before he could snatch me.

He didn't follow me out of the parking lot, and I didn't see his car anymore, but I've been nervous about it all night. Right now I'm holed up in a Burger King, thinking how if he snatches me, no one will know. No one will care.

There's not a single soul in this entire universe who will care.

August 19th, 1:30 a.m., still at Burger King

Remember that essay I wrote where you said I'd used *neighborhood* too many times in one paragraph? You showed me how to use your thesaurus and I told you that the thesaurus was stupid? I told you that if you meant *neighborhood,* you should say *neighborhood* and not use *area* or *district* or *vicinity* or some other lame word that didn't quite mean *neighborhood.* Remember that?

What I didn't tell you was that the thesaurus was lame when it came to finding another word for *neighborhood,* but it was actually an amazing book. I got totally sucked in by some other words on that page. The two I remember are *nefarious* and *necropolis.* Necropolis! What a word! (It means graveyard, you know that, right?) You get this whole feel from *necropolis* that you don't get from *graveyard.* A graveyard seems small. A necropolis seems like an entire *city* of tombstones. It's one of those words you just don't forget.

Nefarious was good, too. Evil. Wicked. Villainous.

Not-fair-as-us. That's how I remember that word.

That day I started making up little snippets of stories that put words I found in the thesaurus together. For example: (*ahem*) Camille, a nefarious backstabber, skipped through Necropolis, the City of Dead, torturing souls with her whiny voice. "I told on you, I told on you, nah-ne-nah, I told on you!"

Don't you love that?

Well, you probably don't, but I do, so what do I care? What I'm telling you is that I miss your thesaurus. I used to sneak it out to recess with me when I didn't have a book to read, then sit in my secret corner of the playground and make up little stories to go with cool new words I found in it.

So why am I telling you all this?

Because I'm working on something, and I need a word for *loose* that rhymes with *endured*.

I need a thesaurus!

And believe me, it's not something I'm going to find in this joint.

August 19th, 4:00 a.m.

Forget *loose* and *endured*. I changed it all around, anyway. I'm finally done (I think). I wanted to finish it before I found a safe place to sleep, but now it's almost daybreak. (I told you poetry was a big waste of time. Ha!)

Anyway, I'm copying it over from the napkins I worked it out on.

Here goes:

NEON IS MY NIGHT-LIGHT

Can the North Star guide the way,
When eyes no longer see it?
Do constellations shine above?
My heart can't quite believe it.
If the aurora borealis
Lights up the northern skies,
It's lost on me,
On city streets,
Neon is my night-light.

Oozing up through sidewalk cracks
Come people of the night.
In black and red, the walking dead,
With ghostly skin and eyes.
Are they after peace or poison?
Will their souls ignite?
Freaks abound,
Tightly wound,
Neon is my night-light.

Blues and pinks and yellows glow,
Cutting through the sky.
Flicker, flutter, flash, and flare,
They eat the night alive.
No one's here to tuck me in,
To ease my fears away.
I dread the dark,
Cold and stark,
But neon is my night-light.

August 19th, 4:00 p.m.

You're not going to believe this!

I am finally, finally, finally AT THE BEACH!

Twelve hours ago I was trying to keep from being scared by writing a *poem* (was I desperate, or what?), and now I'm happy as a clam in sand, baking on the beach. It is *awesome* here! You should see the ocean. It goes on and on forever and ever. No wonder people used to think the world was flat. Or that there was a giant waterfall over the edge of it. It's just hard to imagine all that water, curving on and on around the world clear to what? Australia? Japan? *China?*

And the sand! The sand is hot and soft . . . not gritty at all. It sifts between your toes, and it tickles! And if you dig down a little with your feet, it cools off quick. Wow! I wonder how far *down* sand goes. When does it become rock? (Or crust or magma or whatever the layers of the earth are.) Doesn't matter. What matters is that right now my feet are covered all the way to my ankles and it feels fantastic. Fantabulous!

What a difference twelve hours can make!

Saturday, August 21st

Do you want to hear about my adventure trying to score a swimsuit?

No?

Well, tough. I'm telling you anyway:

Yesterday morning after I'd snagged a cranberry scone from a coffee joint, I sat on a wall looking out at the magnificent Pacific and faced the fact that getting in the water and swimming with dolphins (which I haven't actually *seen* yet) was not something I could do in green corduroy jeans.

I needed a bathing suit.

So I took a little hike to scope out the possibilities and discovered that this is one ritzy neighborhood. Man! I found this area that I guess you'd call a boardwalk—it's got people selling jewelry and souvenirs and Hawaiian clothes from carts and stalls—but there are also restaurants and office buildings and boutiques along both sides of it, and everything is so, so expensive!

I cruised between the buildings, scoping things out, trying to look like I belonged. What a joke, huh? Me with my greasy hair and cap, overloaded backpack, and filthy shoes, looking like I belonged? At least I wasn't wearing my jacket like the bums I saw. Or pushing a whole shopping cart of junk. I'm never going to be one of those bag ladies with a whole shopping cart of junk, you hear me? Never-never-never!

But back to what I was telling you: The people who shop this boardwalk have serious bucks, which is why stores can charge seventy-five dollars for a cruddy bathing suit. Do you know how many days I could eat off of seventy-five bucks?

The price didn't really matter, I guess. I wasn't planning to pay for it anyhow. It was just the idea of people actually spending that much on a bathing suit that shocked me. I made myself get over it, though, and started scoping out the stalls. I didn't stay too long at any of them. I just tried to zero in on the suits that would fit me, then moved on before someone shooed me away.

I felt really self-conscious. Like everyone was looking at me, thinking, Is she a punk? A hood? Is she . . . *homeless*?

One thing punks and hoods and homeless never do is smile. So I always force myself to do just that whenever someone's scoping me out, wondering if I'm trying to lift something. It really throws them off.

So that's what I did on the boardwalk. I even asked some of the hawk-eyed vendors, "How are you today?" like it was perfectly normal for a person in my condition to be pawing through their pricy merchandise.

It didn't make me *feel* any better, though. You should see the people here. I'm not talking about the homeless people (which there are quite a lot of, actually). I'm talking about everybody else. They're not beach bums or surfers or even "California girls." Everybody looks like they're right out of a fashion magazine. Hair. Makeup. Nails. Clothes. I felt like a mangy mutt trotting through a party of poodles.

Not that poodles are bad dogs. Poodles are actually great dogs. They're smart and they're friendly and they've got the most amazing eyelashes ever. Did you know a poodle's eyelashes *have* to be clipped or they get in their eyes? It's like regular hair that just keeps growing and growing.

What's stupid about poodles is not the poodle, it's the people who get ahold of the poodle. All the grooming and fussing and nail painting and *adornments* . . . they turn a dog into a doll. It's ridiculous.

And I kept telling myself that these highly groomed people I was seeing were, in fact, just people. But I didn't feel it inside me. I felt like no matter what I did, I could never fit in. They'd been born with pedigree papers. I was a runaway mutt from the pound.

And, stupid as this is, when you're a mangy mutt rubbing shoulders with prissy poodles, *you're* the one who feels ridiculous.

III

Man, I feel bummed out now. How'd I get on all that, anyway? I was *trying* to tell you a funny story that doesn't have anything to do with dogs.

It actually has to do with *cats*.

And I'm going to try to get in a better mood by powering through and telling you about it. Here goes:

On this ritzy boardwalk they've got all sorts of decorations like flags and metal art and fountains and stuff. They've also got *entertainment*. I saw my first-ever real mariachi band. You know, guys wearing big sombreros and sparkly gaucho outfits, strumming guitars and singing Mexican songs? It was like something out of a movie.

I also saw a man slapping bongos, another man playing some weird drum-shaker things, a woman playing guitar . . . lots of musicians. They had jars out for tips, but they weren't beggars or anything. They seemed to be working together, too, because every once in a while they'd all pick up their stuff and rotate to a new place. It was weird, but they seemed to know where to go and what to do.

Not all of them were musicians. I saw an artist who draws cartoony faces, a juggler, a puppeteer, and a couple of magicians. (One of them was more like a clown with a top hat. He did this stupid trick where he pushed a blue scarf into a tube, did *abracadabra* over it, then pulled out a red scarf. That's all he seemed to know how to do. That, and honk a bike horn.)

So the entertainment wasn't great or anything *except* for this one gypsy-looking dude who had psychic kitties.

Psychic kitties!

Isn't that wild?

They're fortune-telling cats, and this is how it works:

You roll up two dollars and hold them out to one of the cats. The cat takes your money, puts it down behind the booth wall, then hands you a rolled-up piece of paper that has your fortune on it. The cats weren't puppets, either. I watched them pad all around the booth.

That gypsy dude made a *lot* of money. Way more than the musicians. Hey, maybe I should start a booth of my own! My sign could read:

AMAZING!

STUPENDOUS!

EIGHTH WONDER OF THE WORLD!

Come See the One and Only . . .

GYPSY GIRL
and her
SPECTACULAR
PSYCHIC DOGGIES!

Nah. Forget it. It's lame compared to psychic kitties. People expect a dog to be able to retrieve things. Seeing a cat do it is what's weird.

Anyway, that was the funny thing I wanted to tell you. Now back to the bathing suit:

After scoping out the whole boardwalk (and watching psychic kitties in action), I decided to forget trying to score a suit from a cart vendor. They watch like a hawk.

I thought a better plan would be to snag one from a rack that was parked outside one of the boardwalk's surf shops. You know how stores sometimes roll a rack or two outside their front door so you can see the kind of stuff they're selling *inside* their front door? One of those kinds of racks.

I'd passed by this one store about four times and no one was ever out front. So I looked through the bathing suits on the rack and found one that I thought would fit. I spent a long time doing it, too, and no one came out to shoo me away.

I should just have snagged it right then, but I put it at the end of the rack and left, just in case someone was watching me through the tinted store windows.

Over the next couple of hours I passed by that rack at least four more times. The suit was just waiting for me to snag it, and the more I saw it, the more I wanted it. It was blue and sparkly and seemed to be the perfect suit to wear while swimming with dolphins.

This probably won't make sense to you, but I was really nervous about lifting that suit. I don't *like* stealing stuff, believe it or not. I do it, and I'm good at it, but that doesn't mean I *like* it. And normally I don't feel *bad* about it because I steal for survival, not for fun. Usually I'm just so hungry or cold or whatever that I can't be distracted by thinking that what I'm doing is wrong.

But this sparkly blue swimsuit was *not* something I needed for survival.

It was just something I wanted.

I told myself that I'd come a long way to swim with dolphins, that I couldn't exactly do it in my underwear, that there must be a HUGE markup on these bathing suits, and that come on—how much would it actually hurt the store if one went missing?

But it still felt wrong.

That didn't stop me from wanting it, though.

And it didn't stop me from trying to steal it.

It was four o'clock when I finally decided to do it. Everything seemed to be lining up for me: The mariachi band had moved right across the way (and was making a lot of noise with their singing and strumming), I knew a shortcut out of the boardwalk (in case I got chased), and a big group of women had just gone into the store (which meant that people would be busy on the inside and not thinking about the racks outside).

I checked for cops (they walk up and down the boardwalk).

I strolled over to the rack.

But my heart started racing like crazy and I . . . chickened out. I just walked by.

What's the *matter* with you? I asked myself. It's easy! Just grab it and go!

So I went down about six stores, circled back to where I'd started, and looked for cops again.

I strolled over to the rack again.

I reached for the suit. . . .

But at the last second I decided to pull the suit *off* the hanger, and the next thing I knew, hangers were tangled and clanking to the ground, suits were tangled and caught on each other, and people were coming out of the shop.

I panicked. I don't even remember seeing what I was doing. I just grabbed the suit and ran.

I could hear people shouting, and I think someone chased me. I remember stuffing the suit up my shirt to hide it, but other than that, it's all a blur. A weird, dreamlike blur.

When I was sure I was in the clear, I stopped running and caught my breath on the curb between two parked cars. I didn't feel like ha ha, I got away with it. I felt bad. Like I'd crossed the line from survival to crime.

I told myself I was being stupid. Who draws the line? Why is it drawn there? Why isn't it drawn, you know, over *here*? I didn't feel that way when I stole food. Or clothes. Or books. Why was I freaking out about a bathing suit?

I sat on the curb for a long time, trying to figure it out. And when I finally pulled the swimsuit down out of my shirt, I couldn't believe my eyes.

It wasn't the pretty, sparkly blue suit.

It was an ugly green-and-brown one!

With a *skirt*.

And it was way too big!

I felt like that lame magician at the boardwalk. Shove in one color, pull out another.

I got mad. So, *so* mad. It had taken me the whole day to lift a lousy swimsuit, and I'd stolen one that wouldn't even come *close* to fitting.

I shoved it inside my backpack. It was getting late. I was hungry. I couldn't go swimming with dolphins. I had to find something to eat.

Crud.

I had to *steal* something to eat.

After that I had a real lousy night, which I'm not even going to get into. What I *am* going to tell you is that this morning I finally broke down and put that stupid suit on. I had to tie the shoulder straps together in back with a piece of string so it wouldn't fall off, and I felt like a giant piece of ugly seaweed in it, but I put it on and I parked my stuff on the beach like everyone else does. Then I hiked across the sand to the sea.

And you know what?

The water is COLD.

And SO salty.

And full of sand and foam and seaweed.

And, as far as I could see, no dolphins.

Saturday, August 21st, 5:30 p.m.

I was tired of writing. I wrote way too much. All those details. What do they matter? All I had to say was: I met some psychic kitties, I stole a suit, I went swimming.

See? That's all you needed to know.

But the good thing about being sick of writing was that I got up and went back into the water. And now I have one more thing that I want to tell you:

I learned how to bodysurf!

There were some other kids doing it, and I just copied them. Once you get used to the temperature of the water, it's fun. Really fun. My suit filled up like a fishbowl with every wave I caught (no fish, just sand and pebbles and bits of seaweed), but it drained right out (or if there was lots of sand, I dumped it out and went back for more).

I want to go again tomorrow, but I'm through for today. I've got to get completely dry before the sun goes down or I'll be shivering cold tonight.

Monday evening, August 23rd

I am fried! Oh, *man,* am I fried. Burnt to a crisp. "Ow, ooh, eech." That's what I've been saying all day long. My shoulders and my back hurt the worst, but my knees and the tops of my feet are bad, too. They feel like road rash splashed with Tabasco sauce.

Man, am I fried.

7:45 p.m.

Have you ever watched the sun set from the beach? I hate to use this word because you used it WAY too much. (Every time you got excited about something, you'd use this word, and I thought it was really, REALLY corny.)

But now it's the only word that I can find in my head that works.

(See, I need a thesaurus because I don't WANT to use this corny word of yours, but it looks like I'm going to have to.)

Watching the sun set over the ocean is *breathtaking.*

I guess you could watch it and not have your breath taken away, but only if you're not concentrating on what you're watching. If you're actually paying attention, it'll definitely take your breath away. This big, powerful ball of fire dipping slowly past the horizon, shooting flames of color across the sky and blinding light over the ocean. Quivering and shimmering and finally going under.

It makes you feel . . . peaceful.

And grateful.

And awed.

Have you ever watched seagulls fly across the sky at sunset?

High enough to catch rays of the sun,

The bottoms of their wings glowing red,

Rustling in your ears

They make you feel flushed

With a will

To stay free.

Have you ever heard the waves crash against the shore?

At night when the world is still,

Their power, their thunder,

Their command of the Earth

They make you feel humble

And weak

And small.

Have you ever seen the moon mirrored by the sea?

A looking glass of water, of light, of dreams,

It shimmers, reflects,

And washes your mind

It makes you feel lonely

But not

Alone.

I've been trying to figure something out: How did that turn into a poem? *Is* that a poem? It doesn't really fall into any of the categories on your handy-dandy poetry sheet (which is looking mighty tattered at this point). I guess it would be free verse?

What bugs me is, I started telling you about the sunset in regular sentences and then . . . *that* happened.

It was weird.

And I'm not sure if I like it or hate it.

A couple of days later

Every day at about 11:30 there's a parade of scraggly people that goes down the street along the ocean. Some of them wear backpacks, some of them push shopping carts, some of them walk along with nothing at all.

There's one guy in a motorized wheelchair. He wears a black hat and has a little red pennant on his wheelchair that flaps in the air behind him. There are a couple of men in camouflage shirts and others with guitars slung across their backs. It's a weird sight. Like some sort of defeated, retreating army.

The first time I saw them I thought, Man, I'm glad I'm not hanging around them! because I was sure they were a big group of homeless people being run out of town. But the next day I saw them again and I thought, What the heck . . . ? Then I realized that there was only one thing that would motivate an army of homeless to march through the streets together.

Free food!

So I joined the parade (from a respectable distance) and discovered that this town has a rescue wagon!

The woman who runs the rescue wagon is very nice (in a gruff kind of way). She drives into the parking lot of a big church, opens up the side of the truck, and gives a cellophaned sandwich to anyone who wants one. No questions, no sermons, just food!

I met this girl at the rescue wagon yesterday. She's a year older than I am, and she told me her name is Venus.

Like I believe that?

So I told her mine was Gigi and lied to her about everything else, too. I said that I was from Denver and that my parents were a couple of mean drunks, so I was on my way to Oregon to live with my aunt.

"Oregon's awful," she told me. "Rains all the time. And there are no movie stars there like there are around here."

"Movie stars?" I laughed. "Have you ever actually seen any?"

Her eyes got huge. "All the time!" Then she rattled off a list of movie stars that she'd seen and said that one of them had even said hello to her. "I could have touched him, he was that close!"

She told me some more stuff about movie stars, and yeah, I thought she was a big, fat liar. Not like Camille, who knows what she's doing and does it to hurt other people. Like kids I've met at shelters. They tell made-up stories so much that they actually begin to believe them. I guess it's one of those, what do they call them? Defense mechanisms? A way to keep reality from creeping in too close.

Then she asked me, "Where are you staying?"

I shrugged.

"You're not living on the *streets,* are you?" She looked over both shoulders. "Some of these people are truly deranged!"

I shrugged again. Like, no biggie.

"Maybe you can stay at the manor with us," she whispered. "It's exclusive, but I'll ask my mom."

See? She expects me to believe she's living in an exclusive manor? Next she'll be talking about her *servants.*

But I figured hearing about her fantasy life was better than talking to the wall. So I said, "A manor, huh? What's that like?"

"It's *awesome,*" she said. And I was thinking, Yeah, yeah, right. Only then she said, "It's right on the ocean and you can watch the sunrise and the sunset. . . . I've even seen dolphins!"

My head started ping-ponging between *Really?* and *Oh, right.* It couldn't be true, but . . . I still *wanted* to believe her.

"Dolphins?" I asked.

"They swim in little herds!" she told me. "I wish I could swim. Did you ever see that movie?"

"What movie?"

"The one about the boy who lives on a desert island and becomes friends with blue dolphins?"

I shook my head.

"They save him! They swim him back to his parents!"

"Really?"

"Oh, yeah!" she said and then told me the whole plot from beginning to end. When she finally stopped talking, I must have been looking at her a little strangely because she said, "What's the matter? What are you thinking?"

"Nothing," I told her, but I *was* thinking something.

I was thinking that I'd actually found another sea gypsy.

Even if she didn't know how to swim.

I'm going to wrap this up quick because Venus wants me to play cards with her. Basically, her mother said I could come home with them, and it turns out that the "manor" is a big house that's been condemned because of an earthquake. There are signs all over the place that warn you that you'll die if you go inside, but dozens of street people have moved in, and the house sure doesn't *feel* like it's going to fall down the cliff or anything.

I've staked out my own little place on the floor of an upstairs room with some extra blankets that Venus gave me. I'm right next to her, and her mother's off a little to the side. Everyone in this house sized me up quick, said come-on-in, and now they all call me Gigi. One of them even gave me a tube of lotion when she saw how bad my sunburn was.

So I'm feeling very strange. I'm pretending to be someone else, but that someone else almost feels like she belongs.

Next day, 4:00 p.m.

Venus and I spent the day at the pier. She's a total scam artist! She lies about everything, and she shoplifts like crazy! She stole a necklace, some toe rings, a surfboard key ring . . . what's she need a key ring for? I'm sorry I ever told her about us being sea gypsies (which I did when we were playing cards) because she says that's what gypsies do: steal.

She did get us a free ride on the Ferris wheel, though. I'd say the view was breathtaking, but really, I'm not in the mood.

5:00 p.m.

Things are going sour fast. Venus is so nosy! And pushy! She keeps wanting to know what I'm writing in this journal. She even grabbed for it once, but I yanked it away from her.

"What's the big deal?" she wanted to know. "You keep all your secrets in there?"

"No!" I said, then added, "That would be really stupid, wouldn't it?"

She reached for it again. "So why won't you let me see it?"

I knew if I acted too protective of it, she'd get even more curious, so I fanned through it for her and said, "It's just random stuff, see? Poems and notes about—"

"*Poems?* You write *poems?*" She squinted at me like I was the lamest person she'd ever met. "And that's more than notes. That's, like, a whole book!"

I shrugged and stuffed the journal inside my backpack. "I've been on the road awhile."

She scowled. "Homeless people don't keep *journals.*"

"Why do people keep saying that? What *else* is there to do? Besides, I'm not homeless." I smiled at her, trying not to show how mad I was. "I'm a gypsy."

124

"A gypsy," she said, looking at me suspiciously. "And you're on your way to Oregon."

"That's right."

She got in my face. "You're a liar, gypsy-girl."

I stared back at her and said, "Well, you're not a sea gypsy after all. You're just mean." Then I got up and left.

Ha. Guess who I saw walking across the sand just now?

Venus.

She probably thinks I went back to the pier, but I'm right under the house. I'm not hiding or anything. It's big and open under here. There's sand all around and posts that hold up the house.

Hey, maybe I'll go up and snag some blankets while she's gone. I could sleep down here tonight. . . .

But what if there's an earthquake? What if one of these posts gives way? I should probably not even be sitting here.

Yeah, I think I'll find someplace else to hang out. . . .

9:15 p.m.

Venus apologized. And she talked me into coming back inside the manor. We watched the sunset and played cards. She's being nice. Too nice. I think she's scheming a way to steal my journal. I don't get it— it's just a stupid journal.

But the way she's acting is making me feel creepy. I hate not knowing what I'm up against.

Oh, crud. I hear her coming up the stairs.

I think it's Sunday, 4:10 p.m.

It's the journal, all right. She's always watching where I put it. Always asking casual questions about it. I feel like I can't even write anymore. I'm always looking over my shoulder for her. I've even been taking it to bed at night so she won't steal it when I'm asleep.

If she touches it, she's dead meat, you hear me?

Dead phony gypsy meat.

Tuesday, August 31st

I got it back!

I GOT IT BACK!

I hate that phony gypsy! I hate her mother! I hate the whole bunch of them that tried to stop me from beating the crud out of her. It's MY journal. My PRIVATE journal! You can steal my money, you can steal my food, but man, touch my journal and I'm going to beat the crud out of you! It's mine, you hear me?

MINE.

Wednesday, September 1st

So I'm not at the manor anymore. Who cares? I should never have gone there in the first place. Good riddance to all those losers.

I still have to put up with Venus smirking at me when I stand in the rescue-wagon line, though. "Neon is my night-light," she singsonged at me today. "Neon is my night-light."

"Shut up," I told her.

"Make me," she singsonged.

I might have, but I was really hungry and they don't allow brawls by the rescue wagon. I had to make a choice: fight or eat.

I decided to eat.

Still Wednesday, 4:00 p.m.

I'm back at this cave where I stayed last night. It's basically just a hole in the base of a cliff at the edge of the beach. It's not big enough to stand up in, but I like it. The walls are smooth and white. It stays pretty warm, especially with a little fire going.

It's still bugging me about Venus. I don't think she had the chance to read very much of this, but I don't *know* that. What if she found out my real name? What if she makes some anonymous call to social services or something?

But she called me Gigi today, so I'm probably worrying about nothing. And she doesn't read very fast, I know that. But still, this journal is *personal*. Her reading it feels like it did when Gemma Updike yanked down my pants in third grade. Maybe kids on the playground didn't see very much for very long, but for the rest of the time

I went to that school, I walked around embarrassed, wondering who *had* seen what.

Still Wednesday, 9:30 p.m.

I've got a little fire keeping me warm, the sky is crystal clear and twinkling with stars, and the waves crashing onshore sound like the lullaby of the gods. Sometimes I get so caught up in my problems that I forget how amazing the world is.

But not tonight.

Tonight I feel blessed with this moment.

Toes in the sand.

Heart in the stars.

Thursday, September 2nd, 3:00 p.m.

I got drenched last night!

The tide came into the cave, and I must have been zonked out because all of a sudden I was surrounded by freezing water. I grabbed the journal quick, held it high, then bashed my head trying to stand up. Another wave came gushing in and swirled around the cave, then another. Every time I tried to run out, water rushed in. It felt like I was wide awake and half asleep at the same time. Part of my brain was racing, but I was still going, Huh? watching all my earthly possessions get swept away.

I did rescue my backpack, but everything I'd left outside of it was gone. Blanket. Flashlight. Rescue-wagon leftovers. My *bathing* suit. Hand lotion. . . . Good thing I'd bundled up before bed and put my shoes back on or I'd have a lot more to worry about than looking like a drowned rat.

I was still wet when I went to the rescue wagon. Especially my shoes. Venus saw me and said, "Look at you! Were you out swimming with the dolphins?" She singsonged it in a real sarcastic way, so I just pretended she wasn't there and went up to the rescue-wagon window.

"Were you pretending to be a *mermaid*?" she asked, following me.

I got my food and murmured, "Thank you very much," to the rescue-wagon lady.

Venus was right next to me now. "What's that *farting* sound?" she said, like she was totally disgusted. "You are so gross!"

It was my shoes, and it *was* embarrassing. Every step I took, my shoes went *sploosh-thwwwwwt, sploosh-thwwwwwt, sploosh-thwwwwwt. . . .*

The woman who'd given me my food leaned out the rescue-wagon window and growled, "Back off, you uppity homeless brat."

I was so shocked I pointed to myself and said, "Me?"

"No!" She pointed at Venus. "You. I'm tired of you harassin' her. Now back off or I'm not servin' you tomorrow." Then she pointed to two signs posted on the wagon that read:

FOOD SERVICE AT OUR DISCRETION

and

WE RESERVE THE RIGHT TO REFUSE SERVICE

Venus gave her a hate stare but the rescue-wagon woman gave it right back, and finally Venus turned and ran across the parking lot, squealing, "Mama! That witch called me a uppity homeless brat! Mama!"

The rescue-wagon lady scowled and muttered, "Uppity homeless *cry*baby is what you are. . . ." Then, without even looking at me, she slipped another sandwich across the counter and said, "You look like you could use this." Then she pulled the metal window-door closed.

That whole scene actually made me feel pretty good. I've been thinking about why that is, and I'm still not sure. It's not because someone came to my rescue. And it's not that someone called Venus an uppity homeless brat. Even though that *is* really funny. *Uppity* and *homeless* just do not go together, but somehow Venus manages it.

It's also not that I got an extra sandwich and Venus didn't.

So why do I feel so good?

I look gross and have farting shoes, I have no place to sleep and no blankets to sleep under, so why?

Maybe it's because the rescue-wagon lady noticed.

Yes. I think that's it.

It's because for once someone noticed that I *wasn't* the bad one.

I operate under the assumption that people don't notice the good in me. That's just how things always seem to play out. I get blamed, while con-artist kids like Venus and Camille and Gemma get believed.

But the rescue lady noticed.

In the background, just observing, she noticed.

And if *she* noticed, maybe other people in the background, just observing, notice, too.

But if that's true, why don't they step forward like the rescue-wagon lady did?

I feel like I have more questions than answers, but something about one person noticing that I'm *not* the bad one makes me feel better.

Less alone.

Still September 2nd, 6:00 p.m.

You know what's hard to believe?

That it's September.

But it *is* September, and you know what that means:

School's back in session.

It must have started, right? When's Labor Day, anyway? Next Monday? Doesn't matter. School's already started. I can tell by how few kids have been on the beach this week. Which means that right now I'm supposed to be in some junior high somewhere getting an "education."

I hate school. All the mean kids and mind games and stupid busywork.

I really, really, *really* hate school.

But I'm sitting here on the coast of California with palm trees towering above me and sandy beaches as far as I can see, and you know what?

132

I miss school.

What's *wrong* with me?

Friday, September 3rd

I've decided that what's wrong with me is that I don't have a plan. I *had* a plan, but now that I'm where I planned to go, I need a *new* plan.

You know what made me realize this?

A big, ugly brown-and-orange Chevy van.

Sounds stupid I know, but that's because you don't know about the big, ugly brown-and-orange Chevy van my mom and I used to live in. It was *just* like the one I saw today, which is why I did such a fast double take that I threw out my neck. I think I pulled a muscle or put a kink in it. Something. Every time I turn my head to the right now, it hurts.

Our big, ugly brown-and-orange van was really run-down and hard to start, and there were only two seats in it—one for me, one for Mom. The guy Mom got it from had taken the backseats out and had glued orange shag carpet on the walls and the ceiling. He'd even put carpet on the inside of the back doors and across the top of the dash. It was like being inside a big orange fuzz ball.

Mom added strings of beads and silk scarves everywhere she could hang them and hung about six silver crosses over the rearview mirror. When she was done, she giggled and said, "This is so rock 'n' roll!" like she was living a dream.

And since she thought it was cool, *I* thought it was cool. I guess that's how it is when you're eight and a half years old.

For a while it *was* fun, too. No screaming neighbors. No bugs.

No people pounding on the door demanding money. We could drive anywhere, park where we wanted, sleep on the mattress she'd laid in back. . . .

"See, baby?" Mom would say, flipping through a magazine as she kicked back on the mattress. "Who needs a deadbeat job? We've got this comfy rig and the wide open road. I'm into the freedom of this, aren't you?"

Somewhere along the line, that freedom meant I stopped going to school. I didn't really mind. I was happy just being with my mom and a pile of books, living inside our fuzzy orange van.

Still the 3rd, 3:00 p.m.

What *was* my mother thinking? Was she planning to live in a fuzzy orange van forever? She had no job, we had no money, and we were always running on empty.

See? She had no plan.

She used to go out alone and bring food back to the van. But then she started taking me along and using me as a decoy to steal stuff. I'd "trip" and hurt myself while she stuffed her pockets with groceries. Then she'd make a big fuss over me and hustle me out of the store. My mom could score stuff like you wouldn't believe.

I didn't *like* being a decoy, but she always told me how great I'd been. "So dramatic, baby! So *real*. Honestly, we should see about getting you up on a stage!"

Then she started sneaking out at night. She'd tuck me in, and when she thought I was asleep, she'd kiss me on the forehead and whisper, "I'll be right back, baby," then lock up the van and leave.

I used to fall asleep or stay asleep, but one night I got scared and was awake all night, wondering what was taking her so long to come back. Some days it was daybreak before the door squeaked open. She always smelled strange—musty, like burnt rope. Or spicy, like cloves. Or flowery, like too much perfume. Then she'd whisper, "Shh, baby, go back to sleep," and she'd conk out until one or two in the afternoon.

At that point I didn't like living in the van anymore, but I didn't actually *hate* it until Eddie showed up.

Eddie. Why couldn't my mother see what a creep he was? Why did she think hanging out with him was more fun than hanging out with me? She'd actually kick me out of the van! "Don't make a fuss, baby, go play!"

I'd stand outside the van thinking, Play? Where? because we were usually in the parking lot of a supermarket, or just along the side of the road somewhere.

I didn't understand that they were inside doing drugs.

I didn't understand that she didn't want me to see.

I didn't understand that in a weird way she was trying to protect me.

I just knew that because of Eddie I had to play on the side of the road or in the dirty snow of a parking lot.

"Why do you like him?" I'd ask her after he'd gone. "Why do you like him more than me?"

"I don't, baby. Don't be silly," she'd whisper. "He's just helping me through this rough time."

"How? How is he helping?"

She'd give me a dreamy smile, then whisper, "He says he's got a line on a place . . . maybe we'll live there. . . ."

Then she'd be out like a light, and I'd be on my own for the rest of the day.

4:30 p.m.

You probably think my mom was a loser, but she wasn't. She wasn't, you hear me? She was married to my dad, and everything was fine until he got killed in some freak tractor accident.

Yeah, that's what I said, a freak tractor accident.

I don't even remember my dad. Mom showed me his picture over and over, but I don't actually remember *him*. To me, my dad is the picture that my mom kept in a silver locket around her neck. The picture that Mom would look at and cry over.

She didn't have a job before the accident, but afterward she got one cleaning hotel rooms. She didn't make very much money, though, and for years we kept getting kicked out of apartments because there wasn't enough money for food *and* rent. She never *told* me that was the problem, she'd just say, "It's movin' day, baby!" and when I'd complain, she'd laugh and say, "You'll love the new place! It's near the park!" or "Wait 'til you see all the kids!" or "This one's right around the corner from your school! No bus, no fuss! You'll be able to sleep in 'til eight!"

But the new place was always smaller and dirtier than the last place, with bars on more windows and bigger bugs in the kitchen. And every few months angry people would pound on the door, and pretty soon we'd be packing up again.

Eventually I figured it out and I asked her, "Mom, can't you get them to pay you more?"

She just laughed and said, "Oh, baby, baby. That's not the way the world works." Then she kissed me and said, "Don't you worry your pretty head about it. Everything is *fine*."

But one day while I was having my after-school snack, there was a knock on the door and a gruff voice shouted, "Police! Open up!"

Mom grabbed me by the wrist and pulled me into the bedroom. "Hide here," she whispered, pushing me under the bed.

"Why?" I asked. "What's wrong?"

"Shush, baby, shush!" she told me. "Don't make a peep! Stay right there!"

I was quiet, but I didn't stay put. I crawled over to a hole in the wall that my mother had covered up with a drawing I'd done at school. I peeled the picture back and watched and listened, and that's how I found out that my mother was in trouble for stealing money out of hotel rooms.

It took two days for her to come back from the police station.

It took two weeks for us to get kicked out of the apartment.

It was the last real home we ever had.

Still the 3rd, 8:30 p.m.

Don't get me wrong when I say this, okay? But there's something magic about writing. I wish I had a thesaurus because I don't mean good magic. I mean like sorcery. Spell casting. *Strange* magic.

Why? Because when I write, I talk about stuff that I would never normally talk about. I admit stuff that I didn't even realize I felt. I confess stuff that I always just lie about.

It's weird, and it's funny, too. Ironic, I guess, is a better word. Do you know how many people have tried to get me to "open up"? And for all their efforts I've never talked about *any* of this before. Not with social workers, not with kids at school or kids at shelters, not with counselors . . . especially not with counselors. Counselors are the worst! They try to act like they're your friend, but they do it in such a smug way. They sit there like they have all the keys to you but want to casually flip through the whole ring of them before choosing in what order to unlock you.

Their favorite phrase is "I understand." They use it all over the place! For example, they use it at the beginning of interrogations: "Holly, I understand that you are upset because Gemma pulled down your pants, but why do you think pouring motor oil inside her backpack is the way to solve the problem?"

The counselor, of course, assumed I was the one pouring the motor oil (which I was), but I wasn't about to cop to it. I was already wise to their "I understand"'s. If they understood, they'd know that filling up that brat's backpack with motor oil didn't even come *close* to settling the score.

Counselors also like to interject "I understand" into your rages. They think saying "I understand . . ." while you're yelling and trying with everything you've got not to cry will calm you down. How stupid is that? It just makes you madder! How can they "understand" when they haven't even let you finish telling your side of things yet!

But the most irritating way counselors use "I understand" is as a proclamation of their vast knowledge of you. You can have said barely anything, and there they go, telling you, "I understand." They say it all knowingly, with a deep, calm voice like they're channeling God. "I understand."

Give me a break.

I actually think people telling me "I understand" is why I started lying about what happened to my parents. Lying was easy, and a lot less painful than the truth. Oh, social workers always had a big fat file on me, so they knew the real story, but everyone else? I told them the snowstorm story.

I don't know why I haven't been doing that lately. I guess the older I get, the more far-fetched it sounds. But it's still a great story. Way better than the freak-tractor-accident/homeless-junkie story that's the truth.

The kids in your classroom didn't believe the snowstorm story (probably because you opened your big mouth and told them the truth), but kids at other schools, and especially foster and street kids, *love* it. It's so heartwrenching and tragic, you know? Beautiful parents and their beloved daughter separated in the Alps on a skiing vacation. The parents valiantly searching the vast white mountains, desperately calling their daughter's name as night descends and a brutal snowstorm hits. A torrent of wind and snow engulfs the parents, but they don't give up their search. They cling to each other for warmth, calling, "Holly! Holly!" but they are no match for the forces of nature. They die there on the mountain, tears of despair frozen to their cheeks.

"How did you survive?" some kid always asks, eyes bright and wide with wonder.

So I drop my voice and say, "I found a cave. It had an opening, black and narrow, like a wedge of rich chocolate cake." Then I cock an eyebrow and whisper, "And inside it?" and before anyone can say a word, I lurch forward with my hands held high like claws and growl, "*Rrrrrrowrr! A big black bear.*"

Someone usually screams. Most kids gasp. And one quivery voice always asks, "Did he try to kill you?"

But here's where I turn the story around. I tell them, "Actually, no. The bear was sleeping. So I went right up and slept on *him*."

"You *did*?" they gasp.

And real matter-of-factly I say, "I was cold, he was warm. I slept like a bug in a rug." Then, of course, I have to tell them how the next day I skied down the mountain and found out that I was an orphan, but I make that part quick.

I love the snowstorm story.

I don't know why, but it makes me happy.

Saturday, September 4th

I saw that van again today. It was stopped at a red light. It was like seeing a dead person standing right in front of me.

I crossed the intersection and went real slow so I could get a good look inside. Some piggy-eyed woman with greasy hair was driving it, and there was a piggy-eyed boy next to her in the passenger seat. A flowered sheet hung as a curtain behind the seats, but I could see stuff bulging up against it.

It was obvious to me that they were living in that van. Once you've done it yourself, you recognize the signs. There was no orange shag on the dash, so that made it a little less freaky, even though I already knew that it couldn't possibly be the same van as ours. For one thing, our van would never have made it halfway across the country, and for another, the last time I saw our van, it was totaled.

Oh, man. Do I really want to tell you that story?

Oh, crud.

Okay, here goes:

There was this guy parked behind us on the side of a windy road. I remember trees. Lots of trees on both sides of the road. The guy was mad at Eddie and pulled a knife. They started screaming at each other, and Mom shoved me inside the back of the van to get me away from them.

She closed the door, and a few minutes later she came in the front door, shaking like a leaf as she put the key into the ignition. I could hear her whimpering, "Please, God, oh please, God, oh please!" as the motor wheezed and coughed and stuttered and died, over and over again.

Finally, the van fired to life. But before she could put it in gear, the driver-side door flew open and Eddie shoved her over to the passenger seat. He looked wild. Panicked. And he had blood on his hands and clothes.

Mom cried, "What happened?" and he threw the van in gear and yelled, "What do you *think* happened?"

He tore out of there, driving fast and crazy, making me slam against the side of the van as he raced around curves.

"Baby, are you all right?" Mom cried, and when she saw that I was hurt, she climbed between the seats and held me close to her, screaming, "Slow down!" at Eddie.

"Shut up!" he screamed back. Then he looked over his shoulder and shouted, "We wouldn't be in this mess if it wasn't for you!"

I can still see his face. Still hear him shouting. Still feel the van lurching as we catapulted off the road and into a tree.

Mom and I flew forward and crunched hard into the back of the passenger seat.

Eddie flew forward and slammed through the windshield.

For a terrible minute the van teetered, then it shifted and settled onto its side in a gully. Eddie's head was sticking clear through the windshield. There was a lot of blood. I could smell gas. I could hear a tire still spinning in the air.

Mom's eyes were bloodshot. She whimpered and shivered, and then she threw up.

"What are we going to do?" she gasped. "What are we going to *do*?"

I remember my mind racing. Eddie was dead, and the guy he'd fought with was probably dead, too. If we could get away from the van, maybe no one would know we'd been near either of them.

I heaved open the back door and tugged my mom along by the hand.

"What are you doing?" she asked me. "Where are we going?" She looked awful. Thin and sick and petrified with fear.

I pulled her harder and whispered, "It's going to be all right, Mom. We've just got to get out of here."

That was the day she quit pretending to take care of me.

I guess it was also the day that I grew up.

Still Saturday the 4th

I've been staying under the sundeck of a beach house. It's nothing like the manor. It's just a plain one-story, made of painted wood. It's up the coast another twenty minutes or so from the cave, which makes it about a forty-minute walk from the manor. It's quite a hike to the rescue wagon, which is about a mile past the manor, but I don't mind. This house is pretty secluded, which is good since after the weekend I'm going to have to start being careful about who sees me during school hours.

No one has used the deck since I got here, and even though lights come on inside the house, I think they're on a timer. They click on at the same time every night, so I'm guessing that this is somebody's vacation home.

I thought about checking for an unlocked window or door because it would be nice to sleep in a real bed for once, but I decided not to get greedy. You get greedy or start rationalizing why you're doing something and it'll come back and bite you. Mom rationalized a lot. "It's okay, baby. Why should we have to live without the finer things? It's not our fault the tractor killed Daddy, is it? It's not right and it's not fair."

But when she'd lift perfume or nail polish or jewelry, that didn't feel right, either. Not like it did when we'd steal food.

Maybe I'm the one rationalizing now. Maybe stealing food is the same as stealing nail polish. What if hunger just overrides the *other* feeling in your gut? The one that tells you when something's wrong.

What is that, anyway? Where do we get that gut feeling? Do we learn it? Are we born with it? Where does it come from?

I wish I could ask my mom if she really believed what she was saying.

Maybe she was just trying to talk the feeling in her gut away.

Still Saturday, 8:10 p.m.

The shoreline is so graceful. It's like a shallow bay, curving to the left, curving to the right.

Today I sat cross-legged in the sand and faced the ocean. The surf was quiet and the ocean was almost glassy. After just sitting for a while, I started pretending that I was at the bottom of a great, blue, sand-crusted world of water, holding it up like Atlas does with the Earth. I wasn't holding it on my shoulders and back like Atlas, though. I was holding it high, with my arms up, strong and wide, the setting sun floating like a fiery Maraschino cherry in my great blue water world.

It was so strange. My arms weren't even actually up. It was more like my mind wrapped energy around the ocean, sand, and sun and held them safe.

I felt like I'd stepped into a different realm.

A place where I had a purpose.

Where I had power.

THE POWER OF ME

The sand,

   infinite,

      timeless.

The sun,

   fiery,

      commanding.

The ocean,

   yawning,

      merciless.

I held them all, and for just a moment

      I stepped into

  the power

of me.

Monday, September 6th

It was hot yesterday and is today, too. The main beach has been packed with every imaginable size and shape of person having summer's last hurrah. I did a lot of wishing for my ugly swimsuit. The waves have been so nice today. So inviting. Plus, I think my body's thirsty. Maybe it's all the sand or salt air that does it, but no matter how much water I drink, my skin feels thirsty.

Mostly, though, I've been thinking about a plan. I don't *have* one yet, but I know I need one. I'm sick of seeing Venus and her mother at the rescue wagon. I'm sick of walking endlessly through the sand. I'm sick of having nothing to *do*.

Tuesday, September 7th

I saw myself in a mirror today. I look awful! My nose is red and peeling, my face is a deep red-tan, and I have wrinkles! I must have been squinting into the sun a lot because there are little lines of not-tan (or not-as-tan) around my eyes. They don't just look like wrinkles, they *are* wrinkles! My hair's filthy, and I'm still wearing the shirt and corduroy jeans I got from The People's Church. I don't look anything like a gypsy. I look homeless!

I need a plan. I need a plan bad.

September 8th

Okay. Here's my plan:

I find someplace more permanent to live. I get a bunch of books and homeschool myself. I adopt a dog from the pound. I get him a red bandana. (Could be blue.) We hang out together all day, learning stuff and going on field trips together when it's safe (like when other kids are out of school). I'm happy. I'm safe. I'm learning stuff *and* I've got a friend.

That's my plan.

If I really try, I can make it work.

I have to.

Still Wednesday, 2:45 p.m.

I've been thinking that any plan I come up with will revolve around one key thing:

Staying near the rescue wagon.

If I'm hungry, I can't think about anything else. I spend my whole day trying to make the pain in my stomach go away. But since the lady at the rescue wagon's been giving me two sandwiches every day, I haven't had to worry about food.

What's making me nervous, though, is that for the past two days I've been the only school-age kid who's shown up. There's usually Venus and a couple of other younger kids, but yesterday and today it was just me.

I don't think you're allowed to be homeschooled if you don't have a home.

5:30 p.m.

When I was in first grade, there was this boy with a buzz cut named Barry. He was absent so much that kids would ask the teacher, "Did he move? Is he sick? Is he ever coming back?"

The teacher would never really answer, and then one day, like magic, Barry would be back.

"He doesn't *look* like he's been sick," the kids would whisper, and finally one of them would go up to him and ask, "Where *were* you?"

"I was sick," Barry would say with a sniff, but everyone could tell he was faking.

Then some of us started noticing that on the days Barry did come to school, the teacher would take him into the art cubby for a few minutes where we couldn't see them. When they came out, one of two things would happen: Either Barry would sit down at his table and the teacher would act like nothing weird was going on, or Barry would *leave* and the teacher would act like nothing weird was going on.

We all knew that something weird was definitely going on.

This girl named Tiffany figured it out by spying on them. "Lice!" she whispered. "She's checking him for lice!"

I asked my mom about lice when I got home from school. "Oh, baby," she said, "stay away from him!" Then she jumped up and grabbed the phone. "If that boy has lice, he should *not* be in school!"

She made such a fuss. Such a huge fuss. And it seems ironic now that she had absolutely no sympathy for him. Even after talking to about ten different people on the phone and finding out that Barry's father had abandoned the family and that Barry and his five brothers and sisters were living with their mother in a *camp*ground, she still said, "I don't care what their situation is. If the boy has lice, he should not be in school!"

I couldn't get the picture of all those kids living in a tent out of my mind. I thought it sounded like fun. Flashlights, campfires, marshmal-lows, scary stories . . . I thought they were doing it because they liked to camp, not because they had nowhere else to live.

Looking back on it, I understand what was going on.

Barry was the first homeless boy I ever knew.

Thursday, September 9ᵗʰ

I spent the day walking. I wore my backpack and tried to look like I was on my way to school or on my way home from school, but what I was doing was scouting out a new place to live. Under the porch has been fine, but that's because it's summer and it's warm. It gets pretty damp at night, though, and I've been cold a lot. So I walked from here, past the church where the rescue wagon stops, and kept going about an hour, looking the whole time for some better place to live.

You know what I found?

Nothing.

There is no place.

I swear, there's only one cave on this coast, and I about drowned in it.

There are lots of houses, but none of them look boarded up or abandoned. I hate to admit it, but after all the searching I did today, I'm wishing I could still be at the manor. Of course, I can't go back, but why can't there be someplace like the manor that's *not* the manor?

There's probably not, though, because if there was, all the bums I saw today would have found it by now. Once you get off the beach and walk through town or on the street along the beach, it's amazing how many bums there are around here. You see them sleeping on park benches, pushing their carts of junk around, panhandling, or just hanging out, smoking. There doesn't even seem to be a Bum Alley in this town. Just bums scattered everywhere, sort of hanging out with nothing to do.

Still Thursday, 6:30 p.m.

You know what?

I'm MAD!

I'm mad that Venus gets to live in the manor and I don't!

I'm mad that Venus gets to go to school and I don't!

I'm mad that it's foggy!

I'm mad that my clothes are ugly!

I'm mad that my nose is peeling!

I'm mad that I don't have a dog!

I'm mad at my plan! (It stinks!)

I'm mad at my mom!

I'm mad at my dad!

I'm mad at YOU!

I'm mad at everything and everyone.

Why am *I* having to go through this?

What did *I* ever do to deserve this?

It's not fair, you hear me?

IT'S JUST NOT FAIR!

10:05 p.m.

I don't want your SYMPATHY

your PITY

your BAND-AID on my MISERY

I don't want your WELFARE

your "I CARE"

your SHE'S-NOT-LOOKING-NOW-LET'S-STARE

Just give me a CHANCE

a FAIR

FIGHTING

CHANCE

151

Friday, September 10th, 9:15 a.m.

I'm glad I raged yesterday. I feel better today. And I've been thinking that if I could just find a place to live, I really would spend my time reading schoolbooks and studying different subjects.

Even math.

I promise, I'd even study math.

I'm not worried about how to get the books. Lifting them won't be hard. I found a middle school about 20 blocks from here when I was on my endless walk, looking for a place to live.

Once I had the books, I think it would be pretty easy to teach myself. Read the section, do the problems. Read the section, do the problems. How hard is that?

And maybe if I save up all my work, I can turn it in to the super-intendent of schools (or whoever) when I'm 18 and say, "See? I went to school. I just didn't *go* to school." He could check it all over and give me a diploma.

Hmm. Maybe I'll start my own school. It could be called the Sea Gypsy Institute. Or how about Sacred Heart of the Sea Gypsy. Or wait! The GypSea Academy! Ha ha! That's funny! Yeah. The GypSea Academy!

And let's see . . . the school mascot could be the dolphin. Nah. Forget dolphins. The whole time I've been here I haven't even seen one. The school mascot should be a sea dog! Like the ones they have on pirate ships. Scruffy, with perky ears and a happy (yet serious) bark. Yes. That's it. School mascot: sea dog.

And school colors? *Hmm.* How about blue and orange? Blue for the sea, orange for the sun.

And a school motto . . . How about "Ride with the Tide"? Or maybe "Bark at the Shark." Or wait! Here's one you would like: "Sailing the Seas of Success."

Nah, forget that. "Bark at the Shark" is way better.

1:30 p.m.

I've been daydreaming about the GypSea Academy. I know it's stupid, but it was fun to think about, and now I'm in a really great mood because (and you're not going to believe this . . .) I've come up with a *song* for the Academy.

It started as a little chant and just kept building and building. Maybe it's more a lively poem than a song, but I'm calling it the "GypSea Academy *Song*."

Ready or not, here it is:

> Ohhhhh, we're seafarin' gypsies, we learn on our own,
>> *Heigh-ho to school we go!*
> The world is our campus, we haven't a home,
>> *Heigh-ho to school we go!*
> No desks, and no rulers, and no chaperones,
>> *Heigh-ho to school we go!*
> We don't have a lunchroom, so toss us a bone!
>> *Yeaaaaaah . . .*
> We're seafarin' gypsies, each day is a test
>> *Heigh-ho to school we go!*
> Of gettin' to class without an arrest!
>> *Heigh-ho to school we go!*

We pillage supplies, people think we're a pest,

Heigh-ho to school we go!

But we're seafarin' gypsies and we are the best!

WE'RE SEAFARIN' GYPSIES AND WE ARE THE BEST!

Doesn't that put you in the best mood?

Does me.

Friday, 5:30 p.m.

You are not going to believe what happened!

On my way over to the rescue wagon I passed by the manor and what did I see?

Cops!

It was a total shakedown! The cops had Venus's mother and a bunch of the other squatters lined up on the street. They were checking their IDs and frisking them and not letting any of them leave. Then they put them in a paddy wagon that looked like a big armored truck and drove them away.

I know it was childish, but inside I was rooting, Yeah! Haul 'em off! Shut 'em down! Get 'em out of here!

I wasn't the only one, either. I was standing off to the side, in the shadows of a bunch of other spectators, and a lot of them were grumbling "Took them long enough" and "It's about time."

Then the man in front of me said to the woman next to him, "They'll be back. Them or a new group. I give it a week, max."

"Maybe not," the woman replied. "This is the beginning of that sweep they've been planning."

The man snorted. "Yeah, right. And where do you suppose they're sweeping them *to*?"

The lady shook her head. "Anywhere's better than here."

After that I felt sort of sick inside. Sure, I was mad at the people at the manor for siding with Venus, but if I hadn't gotten in a fight with Venus, I'd still be living there. I'd be a squatter, just like them.

It was the word *sweep* that got to me. When I think of sweeping, I think of a broom whisking dirt away. Or I think of that expression about sweeping things under the rug. About taking dirt and hiding it where no one can see it. It doesn't make the dirt go away. It just helps you forget that it's there.

Nobody likes feeling like dirt.

Nobody wants to be swept away.

Nobody wants to be hidden under a rug and forgotten.

It wasn't just the manor that got swept today. It was the whole town, including the church parking lot where the rescue wagon pulls up.

When I arrived, the rescue-wagon woman was hurling wrapped sandwiches through the service window.

"Stop that!" one of the policemen yelled at her.

"You stop it!" she yelled back. "When's the last time you've been hungry, huh?" She hurled another one.

"You're the reason this town's got a problem!" the policeman yelled, coming toward her.

"*I'm* the reason?" She snorted and sidearmed a sandwich. "You've got a skewed view of the world, mister!"

155

"I'm warning you, ma'am. Stop throwing sandwiches or I will have to put you under arrest!"

She stopped and looked at him. "You're going to arrest me for feeding hungry people?"

"No, ma'am. I'm going to arrest you for interfering with police business."

She thought for a second, then managed to rapid-fire about ten sandwiches before he charged the rescue wagon and handcuffed her.

Meanwhile, the church pastor was striding across the parking lot, shouting, "What is the meaning of this? These people are in our care. You have no right to do this! This is private property!"

I couldn't hear what the cop who intercepted him said because I was keeping my distance, looking at all this go down from behind a tree near the church. But the cop showed him some papers and talked a bunch, and even though the pastor argued with him, the cops went ahead and did the same thing they were doing at the manor: checking IDs, letting a few people go, but putting most of them in a paddy wagon.

I lost track of what happened to the rescue-wagon lady. I think they took her away in one of the police cars. But when the parking lot was cleared and the cops were gone, the pastor circled the rescue wagon a couple of times, then closed the service window and went back inside the church.

The rescue wagon might have been closed, but I was pretty sure it wasn't locked. And since it was 2:00 and I hadn't eaten all day, I snuck across the parking lot and tried the back door. It opened with a creak, so I climbed in quick and stuffed my backpack full of as much food as would fit.

Now I'm safely back under the beach house, with enough food for the next few days. But the truth is, I'm worried. If they've shut down the rescue wagon for good, my plan is in the toilet. I'll be back to scrounging food and just surviving.

I wonder how thoroughly they're planning to sweep.

I wonder if they'll check the corners of town.

And the beaches.

And under porches.

Still Friday, 8:30 p.m.

This is really stupid, but I've been thinking about Venus.

What happened when she came home from school? Were there cops waiting for her? Did she freak out when she found out everyone was gone? Is she there now? Does she know what happened to her mother?

I thought about going over to the manor to see if she was all right, but see? That's stupid.

What do I care?

Saturday, September 11th

I walked from here to the manor, to the church, and back. The beaches and boardwalks are packed with people, but I didn't see one homeless person. Not on benches, not at the park, not panhandling at the corners, not at the manor . . . not one.

All of a sudden I'm scared.

What am I going to do if they find me?

And what is my plan so they don't?

Tuesday, September 14th

For three days I've been on the run, cursing the do-gooders who discovered me under the porch. "We want to help you," they said. "You shouldn't be living like this!"

They weren't cops or social workers, but I didn't even have the chance to ask, Uh . . . what do you have in mind? before one of them moved toward me, saying, "There are social programs that help runaways just like you!"

I'd heard enough. I tore up the embankment and cut across the street before they could catch me.

"Wait! We want to help you!" they called after me.

No, you want someone *else* to help me. Some social worker somewhere who helps runaways just like me.

Gee.

How kind.

So all I've been thinking about for the last three days is what I don't have. No home, no family, no food, no *soap* . . . And I've been mad. Really, really mad.

But tonight I was in a market scamming supplies, and just as I'd slid a can of chili into my jacket, one of those gimpy wheelchair guys rolled down my aisle. He was probably about my age, and his mom was pushing him along, putting groceries in a little basket attached to the wheelchair.

The boy's hands were all inward on top of his tray, and his head was lolling to the side as he made gurgling sounds. His mom could have passed for his grandmother, but I don't think she was actually that old. She just *looked* old. Old and tired.

I got out of there, found a safe spot on a cliff overlooking the ocean, and ate cold chili. And all I can think about is how ungrateful I've been. I can walk, I'm healthy. . . . I've got a lot more than I think I do.

Why is what you *do* have so much harder to see than what you don't?

I think it's Friday, but I'm not sure

This road I'm following winds along the coastline, and it's really busy with cars driving at crazy speeds, but other than that it's got nothing. No trees, no grassy areas, no place to *hide*. It's just cliffs down to the sea on one side and cliffs straight up on the other. I don't even know where it's taking me. All I know is I'm going north.

I've run out of my rations from the market. (This is not a complaint, just a fact.) And since I'm hungry and feeling pretty worn out from walking so much and not sleeping enough, I almost said, Sure, when this man pulled over and asked me if I wanted a ride.

A ride would have been SO nice.

But, like I said before, I don't hitchhike.

My mom and I used to hitchhike once in a while when the van wouldn't start, and we never had any problem. People were nice and friendly and helpful. Then came the day that Eddie crashed the van. Mom and I had been hiding out in the woods for hours and hours and hours, but Mom was in a bad way. She was shivering and having the dry heaves, and finally she said, "Baby, I need to get to a doctor."

So we walked back to the road, and Mom put out her thumb. After a while a dark blue SUV pulled over, kicking up a big cloud of dust. The driver rolled down the passenger window and said, "You need a lift back to town?"

He was friendly and nicely dressed, and my mom managed to smile and say, "Yes. Thanks so much!"

I got in back, she climbed in front.

Everything looked tidy. New. And it smelled like vanilla inside the car. I remember really liking the way it smelled.

But after we'd been driving along for a while, the guy reached over and started playing with my mom's hair.

My mom had beautiful hair. Long and thick and curly. That day it was tied back because it really needed washing, but he didn't seem to notice. He reached right over and undid the clip.

I remember thinking that was weird. I remember feeling very uncomfortable.

My mom tried to take the clip back, but he just laughed and put it aside. Then he started stroking her hair, which made me *really* uncomfortable.

My mom whispered, "Stop it!" and pulled away from him.

He clamped a hand around the back of her neck and yanked her toward him, saying, "Don't you tell me to stop."

She whimpered, "Please . . . ," as she looked at me between the seats. "My daughter."

He looked at me in the rearview mirror but didn't let go.

"Please," my mom begged.

"You're hurting her!" I cried and tugged on his arm, trying to get him to let go of her.

He did let go, but his hand flew back and smacked me in the face. He hit me square in the nose, and I remember being freaked out by the amount of blood that was gushing out of it.

My mom screamed when she saw the blood, and it seemed to set something off in him. He started hitting her with the side of his fist, yelling awful stuff as he beat her again and again and again.

"STOP IT!" I screamed and tried to get in between them. My hands were covered with blood from my nose, and when he saw that it was getting all over his clothes and his car, he slammed on the brakes and swerved to the side of the road. "GET OUT!" he shouted, and before we'd even finished stumbling out of the car, he was peeling away.

The first thing Mom did was hold my cheeks and say, "Baby, did he knock out your teeth?"

"No, Mom," I told her. "It's just my nose."

"Did he break it?"

"I don't know." It was tender, but I couldn't tell if it was broken. I pinched it to stop the bleeding.

Mom looked right in my eyes and whispered, "I'm so sorry, baby. I'm so, so sorry."

"Why did he do that?" I asked her. "What did we do wrong?"

"We did nothing wrong." Her hands had moved down to my

shoulders and she said, "Promise me something, baby. Promise me that when you get older, you will never, ever hitchhike."

I nodded, but that wasn't good enough. She shook my shoulders a little and said, "Promise me!"

So I let go of my nose and said, "I promise."

And that's why no matter how tired I am of walking, or how nice or friendly the person acts, I won't hitchhike.

Ever.

It's the only promise she ever asked me to make.

I should stop writing now, but I can't. That day was probably the second worst day of my entire life. The knife fight behind the van. Eddie crashing the van and flying through the window. Hiding in the woods. Seeing my mom so sick. Hitchhiking. Being attacked by a madman . . . It was a nightmare, and I want to get to the end of it. If I can just get to the end of it, maybe I can get it out of my mind.

So, okay. By the time we'd walked into town, my mother was back to shivering and dry heaving. I remember asking her, "Why are you sick again, Mom? You seemed to be better for a while. . . ."

She didn't answer. She was too busy concentrating on finding a doctor.

We wound up in a really scary part of town, with barbed wire and graffiti everywhere, and the building she went to didn't look like a doctor's office at all. It was a tall brick walk-up with bars on the windows and garbage strewn all around.

Inside the front door she planted me in a corner on the floor and said, "Wait right here. Don't go anywhere, you hear me?"

I nodded and I stayed put, but the corner smelled bad, and the people who went up and down the stairs scared me. They looked mean, and I remember thinking that their eyes looked smoggy. Hazy and dirty and yellowed.

Mom took forever to come back, but when she wobbled down the stairs, she told me that she was feeling much better. I was starving and exhausted, and it was dark outside. "Where are we going to sleep?" I asked her, but she collapsed at the foot of the stairs.

"Mom?" I cried. "Mom? Are you all right?"

Her eyes opened about halfway, and that was the first time I noticed that my mom's eyes were smoggy, too. "It's all right, baby," she said. Her voice was airy. Real happy-sounding. "Why don't we sleep right here tonight."

"Here?" I looked around. "Mom, wake up! We can't sleep here . . . !"

But she wouldn't budge.

I didn't know what to do. I wanted to ask someone for help, but there was nobody around. And I had this awful feeling that the people in that big brick building couldn't help me, anyway.

I shook her and I did cry some, but after a while I started looking around and I found a closet. It was a broom closet, so it wasn't very big, but it was better than sleeping out in the hall. So I woke my mom up enough to drag her into it and shut us both inside.

I was very uncomfortable, but I finally fell asleep sitting up.

She didn't seem to mind. She fell asleep with her head in my lap.

I have no idea what day it is

It's been another day of endless walking. Walking and thinking. I hadn't made the connection before, but now I see that the story I made up about Louise K. Palmer has a little of me in it.

Louise waits for her children, and I used to wait for my mom. I used to pretend that she was still alive and that she'd come back for me. I could see her in my mind, arms out, smile big and bright, hair flowing in beautiful curls behind her. "Baby!" she'd cry, running toward me. "Baby, I found you!"

I saw her in my head so often. I heard her voice in my mind. I pretended so hard that I almost believed it. Some days I think I actually did.

Counselors have really tried to get me to talk about my mom, but I've always refused. I didn't like thinking about what had happened or why. I didn't want to face the fact that she was gone forever. I've never talked about any of it, at all, ever.

But now it seems that's all I'm able to do. I finally let myself think about it a little, and talk about it (well, write about it) a little, and now it's like a flood that I just can't stop.

So I walked and thought today, but the truth is, I cried a lot, too. I didn't even try to stop it, or beat myself up for doing it. I just sat on boulders above the pounding surf and let the tears come crashing through.

I didn't know she was a junkie. I just thought she was sick. But she was a junkie, and it's a cold, hard, cruel fact that she loved heroin more than she loved me.

How can anything be that strong? I know she loved me. I know it.

She'd cry her eyes out over the thought of losing me. "You're all I've got left. Please, please, please, God, oh please, she's all I've got left." Then she'd hold me and rock me and whisper, "I love you, baby. I love you so, so much."

So we stayed together, living on the streets. We slept in alleys, back doorways, over heater vents, and if we were really lucky, inside a filthy, closet-size room of a flophouse.

We didn't go to shelters too often because they made my mother very nervous. "They'll take you from me, baby," she'd whisper. "They'll take you from me."

I didn't understand why someone would take me away from my own mother. So one time I asked her, "But why?"

"They'll say I'm a bad mom," she whispered.

I hugged her tight and told her, "But you're a great mom!" and I meant it. With all my heart, I meant it.

I read any book I could get my hands on. It helped me forget my fleabites and itching scalp. Mom didn't seem to care now that we had lice or that we were living among cockroaches and rats. When she wasn't conked out, she spent most of her energy tracking down "the doctor."

I stole food. I stole money. I stole watches, CDs, jewelry. . . . You name it, if it was small enough and I could reach it, I stole it.

"Oh, thank you, baby, thank you!" Mom would say. She'd never eat very much of the food, but she'd take whatever money and valuables I'd snagged and say, "This will help to pay the doctor."

How could I have been so STUPID? I thought I was helping, but all I was doing was helping her score drugs.

All I was doing was helping to kill her.

7:00 p.m.

I don't even know where she's buried.

I don't even know *if* she's buried, or just ashes somewhere.

No one ever told me, and I never asked.

It kills me just to think about.

9:30 p.m.

There's a voice in my head

"Let her go"

There's a hole in my heart

crying, "No"

There's a headwind

A swelling

Strong chains

Demons yelling

There's a voice in my head

"Let her go."

The next day, 8:45 a.m.

I had a talk with my mom last night. I don't know if she heard me, but I felt like she did. I told her I was sorry, and inside I believe that she's sorry, too.

I cried a lot while I was talking to her, but you know what?

Today I feel kind of peaceful inside.

Like the calm after a big storm.

3:00 p.m.

Eureka! I've found BROCCOLI! Fields and fields of broccoli!

I hadn't eaten in two days, but now I'm full of BROCCO-LA-LA-LA-LA-LI!

Who knows what day it is, but . . .

I am on the world's biggest farm! Yesterday I filled up on broccoli, but today I found a field of strawberries. Strawberries! They were yummy with a capital YUM!

Since then I've passed by fields and fields of vegetables. Cauliflower, bell peppers, peas, lettuce, spinach, more broccoli . . . It's a mind-boggling amount of food!

There are no little farmhouses or poultry or pigs. As a matter of fact, there's a *highway* cutting through the middle of this farm. Lots of traffic. Lots of people stooped over in the fields. Lots of irrigation trucks, lots of tractors.

Hmm. I wonder what my dad was doing when the freak tractor accident happened.

I doubt he was harvesting strawberries.

A couple of days later...

My watch stopped working. I think the battery's dead. I'm bugged not knowing what time it is. Bugged way more than I would have thought. It's bad enough not knowing what day it is.

So what have I been doing?

The usual: escaping and surviving.

This particular escaping started because I had to go to the bathroom. And since, like I said, it's farmland around here for as far as you can see, there was no good place to go. No trees, no bushes, no camouflage areas, just fields and fields of vegetables.

The farther I walked down the highway, the more of an emergency it was becoming, so I finally went through a field of (I think) Brussels sprouts over to some portable outhouses. I could see a couple of pickup trucks and a swarm of field workers in the distance, but there were other portable outhouses near them, so I thought I could use one of the nearer ones without being seen.

The outhouses said HUNNY HUT on the outside, which I thought was pretty funny, considering the way they smelled on the inside. But it was an emergency, so I went in, closed the door, and did my business.

Man. It was ripe in there! I tried to hold my breath but wound up having to gulp in a few more. And when I was all done, I tried to shoot out the door, but the door wouldn't open. I frantically turned the lock every which way, but it would not release the door. I rattled, I shook, I twisted, I pushed, but I was trapped.

Calm down, Holly, calm down! I told myself. I tried the door some more. Tried to be calm. Tried to analyze the situation. But the stupid latch wouldn't release and it was SO rancid in there. "Calm down?" I shouted out loud. "I came all this way to suffocate to death in an outhouse? Forget it! No way! Nuh-uh!"

So I sat on the seat and bashed the door with my feet. *Smash! Bash! Crash! Smash! Bash! Crash!* The whole outhouse was shaking!

Smash! Bash! Crash! Smash! Bash! Crash! I whacked it with all my might, and finally, FINALLY the door flew open.

I dove outside, gasping for air, and I landed right in front of a big dusty farmer.

Instead of buying myself some time by yelling at him about the condition of his facilities, I did something really stupid:

I tried to make a break for it.

"Whoa! Whoa!" He grabbed me by the back of my backpack and turned me so I was facing him. "Who are you?"

"Someone who about DIED in there!" I shouted, pointing at his Hunny Hut. "I can't believe you make people use those! They're rancid death traps! I got locked inside!"

He raised an eyebrow at me, holding me at arm's distance. "They're waitin' on the sump truck," he said, "which is behind schedule." He didn't seem mad. Just BIG. Big feet in big dirty boots, big hands, big sweaty trucker hat, big fleshy nose . . . just *big.*

"Let me *go!*" I shouted.

But he didn't. Instead, he walked me over to his big truck and shoved me inside through the driver door, saying, "When I first spotted you, I thought you were a field worker making a bad latrine choice, but you're a runaway, aren't you?"

I dove for the passenger door, but he snagged me by the backpack again and said, "How long you been on the run?" That eyebrow went up again. "And what you been runnin' from?"

I clammed up tight. Like it was any of his business?

He snorted softly and nodded. "Well, it's plain to see you could use a shower and some clean clothes." He shot me a sideways glance. "And a hot meal, most likely."

It's funny what the words *a hot meal* can do to you when you haven't had one in a while. They get your taste buds amped and your saliva flowing. They make you start picturing a table loaded high with meat and potatoes and gravy and vegetables and rolls and butter and pie. And a big pitcher of ice-cold milk. Yes, that's what a hot meal is. None of this fast food stuff. I don't care how hot they serve it, fast food will never qualify as a hot meal.

The bad thing about someone offering you a hot meal is that it can make you drop your defenses, and when you're on the run, it's important to stay suspicious. You don't want to get duped by the lure of meat and potatoes and pie.

But I did quit squirming after that. He drove through the field, over to the swarm of workers, and shouted something in Spanish to one man, who nodded and waved like, Don't sweat it. I got it.

We drove past the workers slowly, then sped up on the dirt road that cut away from the highway between fields. I looked in all directions and realized that no matter which way I ran, there was no place to hide. I was surrounded by fields and fields of low-growing plants.

"I'm Walt, by the way," he told me, looking straight ahead. "Walt Lewis."

I said nothing.

"You'll like my wife. Good cook. Good humor. Good heart."

I still said nothing, but I could see the farmhouse straight ahead. It was yellow and white, with flower beds at the base of the front porch and dormer windows on the second floor.

I love dormer windows. They're very storybook. So between the promise of a hot meal and the sight of dormer windows, he didn't have to yank too hard to get me to follow him inside. And after he explained the situation to his wife, she clucked all over me like a mama hen. "Poor sweet darlin', let's get you into the bath!"

I didn't actually talk to her, but I did turn over all my clothes, then I got in the bathtub. Do you know how long it's been since I've soaked in a bath? Forever! I used to hate baths, but I was stupid. Baths are divine! They're massage therapy for the soul.

And I really needed one! I washed my hair four times before it didn't feel matted to my head anymore, and I had to switch the bathwater three times before it stopped being muddy-looking. I wish I could have just relaxed, but I started worrying about my name being in my jacket. Had she seen it? What if she was calling social services?

Walt's wife came in twice. Once to pass in a change of clothes and say, "I'm Valerie, by the way. I hope these fit'cha. I only had boys, so the choice isn't great, but I've got boxes and boxes in the attic if these don't work." The second time was about an hour later when she knocked and popped her head in, saying, "Supper's about ready."

I still hadn't said anything more to either of them, but when I emerged from the bathroom and came downstairs to the kitchen table, the smell of pot roast and biscuits broke me down. "Oh, that smells so good!" I said, and it came out hoarse. Sort of choked up.

Valerie smiled at me. "Well, look at you!" she said, sounding very pleased. "And those clothes fit you fine!"

They did fit. And they were a good choice: regular jeans and a black T-shirt, with a long-sleeved, button-down work shirt to wear over.

"Have a seat, then," she said, "and let's say grace."

But on my way over to the table a border collie with bright blue eyes came padding toward me. She looked so happy and so sweet that before Walt could finish snapping his fingers and say, "Chia, corner," I was down on my knees, letting her love me up with doggie kisses.

Valerie laughed, and Walt did, too, but they made me wash my hands and face again before eating.

Dinner was great, and they were nice, but I didn't say a word. I did shrug and shake my head some when they asked me questions, but when they started trying to find out more about why I was on my own, I quit making any kind of response at all. I just ate.

Nobody from social services came pounding on the door, and Valerie set me up in a room, like of course I was going to spend the night. The bed was big and soft, with feathery pillows, and there were all my clothes, clean and folded at the foot of it.

I fell asleep right away, but in the middle of the night something spooked me awake. A noise. Footsteps *inside* my room.

I clicked on the light quick and laughed when I saw it was Chia. "Hi, girl!" I whispered, then got back in bed and patted the covers. "Want to sleep up here with me?"

She jumped onto the bed and lay down against me. I put my arm around her, and for one brief, floating minute I felt so, *so* happy.

Then I started having dangerous thoughts:

What if Walt and Valerie could become my foster parents? I could help around the farm. I could go to school. Or if there weren't schools around, maybe Valerie would homeschool me. I'd be a good student. I'd try hard. I'd be helpful and grateful, and Chia could sleep on my bed every night.

I'd have a dog. . . .

I'd have a home. . . .

I'd have a family. . . .

Early the next morning Chia nudged me awake. I let her out of the room and heard little clinking noises coming from the kitchen. So I went downstairs, where I found Walt reading the paper and drinking coffee at the table while Valerie fried eggs at the stove. I stepped inside the kitchen and asked, "Do you need any help?"

Valerie practically dropped her spatula, and I must have startled Walt, too, because he jerked and spilled a little coffee.

Valerie laughed and said, "Well, good morning! You're up early."

There was toast sitting in the toaster so I went over and said, "Would you like me to butter these?"

"Sure!" Valerie said, handing me a dish of butter. "That'd be great."

But something was wrong. And it wasn't just that I was suddenly talking to them. Valerie was nervous, and I was pretty sure I knew why.

I didn't say, You called social services, didn't you. I just ate breakfast and then excused myself to use the bathroom. But what I really did was hide around the corner, and when they thought I was gone, Valerie whispered, "I feel like I'm betraying her! She seems like such a sweet, scared child. . . ."

I heard the paper rustle and Walt's voice say, "She'll run, Valerie. She'll run and wind up in the condition I found her in all over again."

"Maybe she can stay here with us."

"Val . . . ," he warned, "we're too old for that. And we can't give her what she needs."

"What the girl needs is love!"

I heard the paper snap and Walt's chair grind back. "What she needs is a family and friends and a place to go to school. She'll be in good hands, Val. The woman sounded very nice. We're doing the right thing."

"They're coming at eleven?"

"Around eleven. That's what she said."

I was already backing away from the kitchen when I heard him say, "Tiller's can't get me that tractor part until next week, but I located one in Santa Barbara. I'll be taking a quick trip up there this morning after I make the rounds."

"But . . . what about the girl?" Valerie whispered. "What if she tries to run?"

"She'll be fine. Just keep her busy. I'll be back before eleven. And if she does try to run, call Hector on his cell. He'll spot her and bring her in."

I hurried away, then made a noisy walk back to the kitchen. "Do you mind," I asked them, "if I go back to bed? I . . . I'm still really tired."

"No, of course not," Valerie said.

So I went upstairs, stuffed the bed with pillows, shoved my things into my backpack, and climbed out the dormer window. It wasn't hard getting down because the top floor wasn't as wide as the bottom floor and there were posts and window ledges to hold on to.

I could think of only one way off the farm without being seen: Walt's truck. I managed to get to it before he did, but there was no place to hide in the bed. It was a 4-door, though, so I sneaked inside the cab through a back door and hid on the floor, camouflaging myself with a tattered tarp that was lying there.

I was still rustling around when the driver's door flew open.

I held my breath and waited, but nobody yanked me out of the truck. Instead, it fired up and rolled away.

Walt stopped and talked to several people before he finally hit the highway. And then he turned on the radio, and we just flew down the road for about an hour before he parked the truck and got out.

I gave it a few minutes, then looked out the window. We were at some tractor facility. But there were trees and shrubs right across the parking lot, so the first chance I got, I snuck out of the truck, hurried over to the bushes, then watched and waited.

It took only about ten minutes for Walt to saunter back to the truck. He had a box in his hands and looked like he was whistling.

"Have a nice life," I whispered as he drove off. I meant it to be sarcastic, but there was a big lump in my throat when I said it. On the outside I was kissing them off, but on the inside I was thinking that maybe I should have told them why I didn't want to go back into "the system."

Maybe I should have asked them to let me stay with them.

Maybe Valerie would have been able to talk him into it.

I felt like a stray dog that had wandered onto their property. A stray that half the family wanted to keep and the other half wanted to take to the pound.

Why didn't I wag?

Why didn't I beg?

Why didn't I *try*?

But I didn't.

And it's too late now.

A few days later...

No one's tracked me down, so that's good. And this town where I've landed is very easygoing. So I should be happier than I am, but something's really bugging me. I've been thinking about it on and off since I wrote what happened with Walt and Valerie, and I don't like the way it makes me feel.

It has to do with the first foster family they put me with after Mom died. Not the emergency-care family, the first permanent family.

I walked in the front door hating them. I'd been told they'd be like a new mother and dad. Well, she was not my mother and he was not my father. I didn't want to call them Mom and Dad. I didn't want to be their daughter. I didn't want to bathe every night and wear T-shirts with sparkly letters or brand-new jeans.

I hated that they were so cheerful when I was so sad. I hated that they were so nice to me and gave me all the things my mother couldn't, especially during the time when we were living on the streets. I hated that they called me sweetheart. I hated the clean sheets and the unicorn wallpaper and the Minnie Mouse night-light.

So one day I smashed it all and ripped it all and kicked it all and screamed, "I hate you, I hate you, I hate you!" at the top of my lungs.

When they got rid of me, I was glad.

Good riddance to them.

I never really thought about them again. Never looked back. I just went from home to home, hating everyone I met and storing up a deep, dark reserve of anger. Anger that I started needing for survival when they quit putting me into "happy homes." Anger I needed to fight back against people who tried to Sani-Flush me.

Or worse.

But I look inside myself now and wonder: Where is all that anger? It's still there when I think about the Fisks or the Benders, but it's not the big dark wall that used to be everywhere, all the time.

And I can't believe I'm saying this, but unicorn wallpaper sounds . . . nice.

Clean sheets are really . . . nice.

A bath every night would be so . . . nice.

Something feels different inside and I don't really know why.

Is it just the passage of time?

No, that can't be it. A lot of time passed before, but nothing got better. It just got worse.

So I don't know. But it is a strange feeling. It's like I've solved something inside me, but I don't really understand how, or even what the puzzle was.

October 4th

I can't believe it's *October*. It doesn't feel anything like fall. It's sunny and warm and I like this kicked-back town. People are friendly but mind their own business. It must be a pretty big city, but it doesn't *feel* that way. Lots of trees, lots of flowers, lots of green space.

I've been sleeping near a lagoon. At least I think that's what it is. It's not big enough to be a lake, and there's reedy grass growing out of it near the shores.

There's a path that goes around the lagoon that people use for jogging or riding bikes or pedaling these bright yellow "Rent a Surrey" contraptions. The surreys must be hard to steer because I've seen about six of them go off the path. Nothing serious. The riders just push them back on the path and keep going.

This area where I'm staying is perfect. It's a little wedge of land between the railroad tracks and the freeway on-ramp. It sounds like it'd be noisy, but it's not bad. And I really like the trees. They're tall, with smooth white bark and droopy branches that have long, spear-shaped leaves. I think they're eucalyptus trees. They smell good, and the dropped leaves make a nice soft pad to sleep on.

It took me a few days to figure out that I was near the ocean. It seems stupid now, but I kept walking in the opposite direction because that's where the food stores are. But yesterday I discovered that I am indeed still a sea gypsy!

The beach here is different from the one I was at before. There's lots of driftwood and seaweed on it, and the sand is not as white or as fine. There's actually *tar* in it. I have little black chunks of tar all over my shoes from walking across the sand.

There's also a long stretch of park that runs alongside the beach. It must be two miles long! It has a bike path on one side, a sidewalk on the other, and public bathrooms in between. It's very comfortable. Very relaxed.

I'd like to stay here.

It feels like it could be home.

October 6th, Wednesday

It is my lucky day! There's an organic market right down the road, and I was on my way out of it (after pocketing an apple) when I noticed a five-dollar bill on the ground. It was folded in half twice, and when I unfolded it, I discovered that it wasn't just a five. It was a five and a ten and two ones! Seventeen bucks!

I'm rich!

A couple of days later (I'm pretty sure it's Friday)

I am so set up, it's great! Good thing I'm not going anywhere or I'd need a shopping cart! (And I swore I'd never, ever be a Shopping Cart Gypsy!)

Ever since I got here, I've had the best luck. First I find this wonderful little wedge of land that's comfortable, has perfect camouflage, and none of the bums around here seem to know about. (And there are quite a few bums around, by the way.)

Then I find that wad of money outside the store, and THEN I find some stuff that I'm sure was abandoned. I stumbled across it when I ducked behind some shrubs to ditch a cop who I thought had his eye on me.

After I was sure the coast was clear, I tried to figure out how the stuff got there. It wasn't really hidden. It was more just dropped. Maybe some guy was living under the overpass and it all fell down the embankment? Maybe he shoved it over the edge because he didn't want anyone to find it and then something happened to him? Maybe he got drunk and forgot where he stashed it?

I have no idea, but it sure looked abandoned, so before someone else claimed it, I hauled it all back to my camp.

I scored two big garbage sacks full of crushed aluminum cans (soon to be recycle money!), a grocery bag with cans of food, a small (but sharp) can opener, a dense foam mat, and a sleeping bag.

Can you believe that?

A *sleeping* bag.

It's not the roll-up kind, either. It's the stuff-in-the-sack kind, full of soft, fluffy feathers. It stinks a little, but it's so warm! And the mat may not look too comfortable, but it insulates you from the ground, which is wonderful. I wasn't cold at *all* last night (and usually I'm shivery from about 3 a.m. on).

Still Friday, quite a while later . . .

I tracked down a recycle center! It's about a mile from here, behind a supermarket. I found it by following a homeless guy who was pushing a shopping cart of bottles and cans. Took me right to it.

The center closes at four, so I don't have time to go back today, but tomorrow I get even richer!

Saturday the 9th

I may be in trouble. I got going early this morning and hauled the first sack of crushed aluminum cans all the way to the recycle center. I wanted to get there when they opened because I had two trips to make. Plus, most people don't get moving as early on Saturday as they do during the week, and the fewer people that saw me hauling a sack of garbage over my shoulder, the better.

What I didn't know was that this recycle center is a big morning-time homeless hangout. There must have been fifteen bums there! Their shopping carts were parked all over the place, and there were a few dilapidated bicycles leaning against the recycle trailer. The bums weren't there to turn in bottles and cans, either. They were just drinking coffee and smoking cigarettes, shooting the breeze with the guy who works at the center.

I wanted to leave and come back later, but I had no place to go. Plus, I had this sack of cans that I was more than ready to unload. It was heavy, and I was thirsty and tired from lugging it so far.

So I took a deep breath and went up to the recycle guy, who was sitting in a chair inside the trailer. He looked homeless himself: tan, oily hair, worn jeans, bad teeth, dirty tennis shoes. . . .

I made a mental note to buy myself a toothbrush, then asked, "Can I turn these in now?"

"Sure, sure!" he said, standing up. He came out of the trailer and handed me a tall wire-mesh container, saying, "Looks heavy. You got glass?"

"Aluminum," I answered, swinging the sack off my shoulder.

I opened the sack and let the cans cascade into the container, but before I was even done, he plucked out one of the cans and said, "Where'd you get these?"

I had a lie all ready for a question like this, but I was expecting to have to use it on a cop, not some homeless-looking recycle-center attendant. "Where'd I *get* them?" I asked. "My scout troop's been collecting them for months."

He eyed me suspiciously and said, "Your scout troop." Then he looked around and asked, "If it's for your scout troop, why you here by yourself?"

183

The other homeless guys were moving in closer and I really wanted to bolt out of there, but I tried to keep my cool as I said, "I got assigned, all right?"

"Hmm," he said, and swung the container of cans onto the scale.

"You think they're Hog's?" one of the bums asked the recycle guy.

The recycle guy didn't answer. Instead, he went into his recycle trailer and brought out an uncrushed aluminum can. "Crush this for me, would you?"

I took a quick look at the cans I'd dumped into the container. I knew they were crushed tight, but now I noticed that every one of them was crushed the same, with a sort of twist in the middle. There was no way I could duplicate that.

"You always give your customers the third degree like this?" I snapped. "I'm in charge of delivering cans, not smashing them. If it's any of your business."

Other bums were pawing through the container now, saying, "These are Hog's, Mac."

"Yeah, Mac. No one does a can like that."

"Get back, you vultures!" I shouted. "They're *my* cans! Quit picking them apart!"

The recycle guy checked the weight, swung the basket off, and headed for his calculator inside the trailer, saying, "When a guy gets thrown in the slammer a few days and comes out finding his stuff missin', he tends to accuse eeeverybody he knows."

"Yeah," one of the bums grumbled. "And all this time it's been some *girl* scout. Imagine that."

There was a little chorus of hobo sniggering, and one guy said,

"Little girl, you don't want to be messin' with Hog *or* his dog. They'll tear you into little bite-size pieces and roast you."

"And he ain't talkin' s'mores!" another bum said, which caused a full-blown chorus of hobo laughter.

"You know what?" I said. "I'm going to call the police." I turned to the recycle guy. "Does your boss know you're running a homeless hangout here? Does he know you're intimidating customers? *Threatening* customers? You think me or anyone I know is ever coming back here to do business? I'm telling my leader and my teachers and my parents exactly what I had to go through to turn in these cans, and they're going to—"

"All right, all right!" he said, stamping a slip of paper and handing it to me. "Here's your voucher. Go redeem it in the market."

"You're givin' it to her?" one of the bums said. "Hog's gonna blow a gasket!"

He signaled something to them that I didn't catch. I was too busy racing out of there.

Inside the store I kept my eyes open for the men from the recycle center, but none of them seemed to be following me. So I grabbed a toothbrush and a travel-size toothpaste, and since one of the public bathrooms near the beach has pay showers, I also picked up a travel-size shampoo and conditioner.

Meanwhile, my stomach was distracting me because I could smell roasting chickens. I don't know why the store was roasting chickens so early but they were, and my mouth was pouring saliva!

So I wandered back to the deli, hoping that they were passing out samples, but they weren't. But then I noticed that a whole chicken was only $4.50! So I thought, What the heck! and grabbed one (they were in these thick, see-through, to-go bags under a heating lamp). I also picked up a loaf of soft potato bread. The combination sounded SO good.

And yes, I actually paid for the chicken and the bread. I was planning to pay for everything, but at the last minute I slipped the shampoo and stuff in my pockets. Habit, I guess.

I still hadn't seen any of the guys from the recycle center, but as I was going through the checkout line, I spotted a pack of them out in front of the store.

No one had to tell me what they were waiting for:

Me!

So I handed over my recycle voucher to pay for my chicken and bread, got the change (which was almost $15), asked the checker if I could go back through the store to get some napkins at the deli (she said, "Sure"), walked around until I saw an EXIT sign over a door by the meat department, pushed through that, and made a beeline past a bunch of crates and boxes to an open roll-up door.

I looked left and right before stepping outside, then got away from there as quick as I could. I took backstreets and kept a sharp eye out for homeless guys trailing me. The aroma of roasted chicken was driving me crazy, but I didn't stop for anything until I was safely home.

And now that I've been here awhile and have eaten a scrumptious meal of chicken and bread, I'm worried about a lot of things: Are those creeps at the recycle center going to tell that Hog guy about me? (Of course they are. That way he'll stop shaking *them* down.) Will all the homeless guys in town be on the lookout for me now? What if they set up some hobo network to find me? (Okay, that sounds really far-fetched. But these guys seemed like a pack of rotten-toothed hyenas, and I'm feeling really nervous.)

I'm also feeling kind of confused. "Conflicted," if you want to psychobabble. Here I've snagged some homeless guy's sleeping bag, I'm using his mat, eating his food, cashing in his cans. . . . He's *homeless*. How low can you go?

Right now I'm thinking I should put it all back where I found it.

But what kind of guy is named Hog? And the recycle guy said he'd been in jail like it was no big deal. Like it happened a lot.

So if this Hog guy's a *criminal,* he probably *stole* the sleeping bag and stuff from someone else, right? Why *would* I return it to him when it wasn't really his in the first place?

Am I rationalizing?

Is this like the swimsuit?

Like my mother stealing lipstick?

Or does this qualify as survival?

Sunday, October 10th

Maybe I am rationalizing, but I can't seem to bring myself to put the stuff back. I love this sleeping bag.

But I keep worrying about what will happen if Hog catches me.

What then?

I hate feeling this paranoid. I can't enjoy *any*thing. There's no school today, kids are everywhere, there's an amazing arts and crafts fair down by the beach . . . it's a perfect day to just cruise around without having to worry about cops questioning me. But with this stupid Hog problem, I'm constantly looking over my shoulder.

I hate living like this. I hate it, I hate it, I hate it!

Maybe I should return Hog's stuff.

Monday, October 11th

Took a shower in that bathroom near the beach (used the hand dryer as a hair dryer—aah!), scored an amazing submarine sandwich (and paid for a quart of milk), and saw Hog.

I'm sure it was him. Long salt-and-cinnamon hair and beard. Ruddy, glowery face. Beefy body. Grimy from head to toe. He was riding a typical homeless-guy bike but with chopper-style handlebars going out to an extended front wheel. He had two black half-full Hefty sacks strapped over the back fender like saddlebags, and a pit bull–rottweiler mix on a rope leash running alongside.

I'm not sure if he got his name from his size, his filth, or his bike, but whichever, I was pretty sure it was him, and then I watched him paw through a trash can and demolish aluminum cans and *knew* it was him. Twist, crunch! Twist, crunch! Bare-handed. Brutal. *Fast.*

I'm glad I saw him because it's good to know what you're avoiding.

It's also good to know that his dog is not some sweet, cute, panty thing. I saw him lunge at two joggers in less than five minutes. He's a brute. Just like his owner, but with drool.

So now I don't feel as guilty for keeping his stuff, but inside I've gone from paranoid to petrified.

Tuesday, late afternoon

I got the bright idea that cashing in the second sack of cans would be a smart thing to do. It would transform big, bulky evidence into compact bills for future survival needs.

So I located another recycle center (in the phone book—it's about five miles from here), figured out the bus schedule to get me there (there's a stop two blocks from it—seemed easy), hauled the second sack of cans clear to the bus stop, rode the bus through endless stops clear across town, dragged that sack around until I finally found the recycle center, and . . . it was closed! *Closed.* Every Monday and Tuesday they're closed! What kind of stupid business is that?

And the worst part is, when I got off the bus on the way home, I crossed paths with about five different homeless guys. None of them followed me or even seemed to pay much attention to me, but street people are a lot slyer than you think. If they're not wasted on drugs or booze, they're watching people. Sizing them up. Scamming.

It's easy for them to do.

Nobody wants to look a homeless guy in the eye.

Tuesday night

A sweet-looking little old Mexican lady busted me lifting boiled eggs from her market. She grabbed me by the arm and frisked me until she found them in my pocket. She was strong! I was afraid she was going to call the police, but she just scolded me in Spanish and shoved me out the door.

I'm still embarrassed.

Busted by a little old lady.

Wednesday

Where did my good luck go? I was sitting at the bus stop with the second sack of cans between my feet when guess who came moseying my way, trolling through trash bins for cans?

Hog and his dog.

"Come on, bus, come *on,*" I whispered because he was getting closer and closer, and bus stops around here are made out of Plexiglas that you can see right through.

When the bus finally pulled up, Hog and his dog were only about 30 feet away, digging through a trash bin on the grass between the street and the beach.

The bus doors opened, so I clanked onboard with my cans and dove into the first open seat. I stared at the doors, hoping, *praying,* that Hog wouldn't charge onto the bus.

The doors closed.

We pulled away.

I started breathing again and looked out the window.

Hog was staring right at me.

Two stops later

Okay, it's stupid that I've hauled this out to write in again, but I'm freaking out! What if Hog's arranging a welcoming committee for me at the other recycle center? He must've figured out where I'm going with this fat sack of cans, right?

What if he's putting the pedal to the metal himself? At the rate this bus is going, he could ride his chopper bike to the recycle center and greet me personally. Then what? I could abandon the cans, but he's still going to want his sleeping bag. And the money from the other cans (which I only have about half of left). And his sack of food (which is also not exactly all there . . .).

What am I going to do?

Riding the bus home

I'm rich! No Hog waiting for me . . . just a really nice retired marine sitting in the trailer reading a magazine, waiting for people to come along with their recyclables.

I cashed in the voucher, no problem, and splurged on a new flashlight and batteries. The store had a camera counter, and on a whim I asked whether they had batteries for watches and they did! The lady was real nice, too. She said they weren't supposed to install batteries for customers anymore, but when she saw me fumbling with the jeweler's tools she'd lent me, she said, "Here. Don't tell anyone," and did it for me.

I also (*ahem*) acquired a book. It's about three single mothers who run a kiddie day care but are secretly a ring of diamond thieves. (Their ex-husbands are diamond dealers, and the women are getting back at them.) It might be really good or really stupid, but I'm dying for something to read, and the only other books they carried were repulsive romances.

I'd start reading now, but I don't want to miss my stop.

Actually, I *do* plan to miss my stop. I'm going one stop past the beach stop just in case Hog and his dog are watching and waiting for me.

1:15 p.m.

I'm freaking out again.

Who says I'm paranoid? We just pulled away from the beach bus stop, and guess who was there?

Hog and his dog and a bunch of homeless hyenas!

The place was teeming with bums!

They weren't waiting right there *at* the stop. They were actually pretty inconspicuous, waiting in the distance, camouflaged by trees or trash cans. . . . But once I spotted Hog, I started seeing the rest of them. They weren't there because it's the beach stop and a really cool place to hang out, either.

They were waiting for me.

How do I know?

Well, when the bus pulled up to the stop, Hog whistled between his fingers, and the hyenas who were awake turned and watched the people who got off the bus. The more I think about this, the creepier it gets. Can you imagine being chased down by homeless people? It's like ghouls from the garbage instead of the grave! All tattered and dirty and staggering around . . .

This is too weird to believe!

What am I going to do?

I'm living in a freakin' nightmare!

Saturday the 16th

I'm on the run again. I'm so tired of hiding and lying and stealing. I'm so sick of getting nowhere and feeling like no one.

What's the use?

Why am I doing this?

I have no plan.

I have no place.

I have no purpose.

I want more than to just survive.

Just surviving gets you nowhere.

11:30 p.m.

GOODBYE

Smoke wafting skyward

Thinning, then disappearing

A flame's wave goodbye

I think it's Wednesday, but I'm not sure

I'm glad I had that book to read. It turned out to be really funny. The three women were hilarious but in a real tough-as-nails kind of way. Their ex-husbands never stood a chance. It was a revenge-against-betrayal story. Not deep or allegorical or metaphorical or anything educationorical (ha ha!), but I liked it. I liked it a lot.

So I'm not feeling as bummed as I was, but I definitely need a new plan. A *real* plan. Starting with a better place to live than under this overpass. I'm far enough away from Hog where I'm not worried about him anymore. (I don't know what direction I went, but I stowed away in a musty, humid *mushroom* truck for almost two hours, which seemed plenty long enough.)

There are about six people camping under this overpass, and they're already working on my nerves. It's not because they're drinking or swearing or talking to themselves like drugged-out lunatics. They're bugging me because they act so superior. Here they sleep on cardboard mats under a bridge, they're filthy from head to toe, they wear shoes that don't match (and two of them have only one sock), they smoke cigarettes and pee against the wall . . . and they act like everyone besides them is stupid. It's unbelievable.

To be fair, there is one guy who doesn't act that way, but he's actually the one who creeps me out the most. His name's Martin and he doesn't say much, but I catch him checking me over a lot. He has dozens of snake tattoos coiling around his arms and around his neck and probably around his whole body, which is just nasty. Why would anyone wrap themselves in snakes?

I keep telling myself that being here is better than being hunted

194

down by a pack of homeless hyenas, but I really, really, really miss my little spot among the eucalyptus trees. I didn't have any choice about leaving, though. I barely got away from Hog in time.

The good news is that I managed to escape with the sleeping bag, so at least I've been warm at night. I can actually stuff the sleeping bag inside my backpack. Not much else fits, but carrying a sleeping bag under your arm or even strapping it onto your pack is just too much of a giveaway that you're living on the road.

I'm in a town that's a lot like the area where Walt and Valerie live. Lots of fields. Lots of farm workers. Broccoli everywhere. The difference is, there are also big areas with shopping malls and auto malls and condominiums. Imagine miles and miles of land cut into a patchwork of farm fields, and scattered throughout the patchwork are cement squares packed from edge to edge with stores or houses or cars. It's like, one by one, the farmers in town are getting tired of tilling the earth and are paving it over instead.

The nice thing is that if you get desperate, you can just go out into the fields at night and eat broccoli or Brussels sprouts or whatever you find out there. I mentioned that to Charlene, one of the women who's living under this overpass, but she snorted and said, "Ferget that. I ain't eatin' no pesticides." She took a deep drag off her cigarette and smirked at me like I was ignorant beyond belief. "If it'll kill bugs, it'll kill *you*."

I think I'm going to go scout around.

See if I can find a school.

Lift some books.

Something.

A few days later

I left to find a school and I wound up at the movies. It was a spur-of-the-moment backdoor sneak-in, but I've been here for *days* now. It's one of those big multiplex theaters with an upstairs, a downstairs, bathrooms, a video arcade, and a half-mile snack counter.

I've been living off popcorn and soda. At first I scarfed up what people left around after the movie was over, but then I discovered that they give free refills on their "Titanic Tub" and "Colossal Coke," so I snagged one of each of those off the floor and have been getting refills ever since.

At night I've been sleeping behind a screen in one of the downstairs theaters. Most of the theaters in this multiplex have a screen flat against the wall, but two of them have a door behind the screen that leads to an old-fashioned stage area. Maybe they were the original theaters and the rest of this multiplex was built up around them. I don't know. And really, I don't care! No one ever comes back here, and it's easy to sneak in and out when the lights first come down because everyone's blind for a minute.

It's also cool because I can leave all my stuff back there and pretend to be an everyday moviegoer with nothing to lug around but popcorn and soda.

So I'm actually having fun. I've seen more movies in the last few days than I've seen in my whole life. Ditto on the popcorn! And it's really easy moving around this place. Nobody checks for ticket stubs or says, "Hey, haven't you gotten a bunch of refills already?" There are different people working the snack counter every few hours, so it's like, "Refill? Sure!"

This is the life, man.

A few more days later

I got busted by the "manager." The pimply-faced twerp. I don't think he's old enough to realize I'm too young to be living in a movie theater. Which makes him pretty stupid, but I guess that works out fine for me. He even threw my sleeping bag out after me, with the classic, "And don't you come back!"

Pimply-faced moronic twerp.

Oh, well. I was sick of popcorn, anyway. And stupid movies. And no sunlight.

Now that I'm outside again, there's sunlight but no sun*shine*. It's cloudy. And cold. What happened? You go to the movies and it's summer, you come out and it's fall.

I wonder what day it is.

The 25th of October?!?!

No wonder it's cloudy! No wonder it's cold! It's almost NOVEMBER!

Enough fooling around.

I need a plan!

One that'll get me through the winter.

And I need to come up with it quick!

4:00 p.m.

I found a school today. A junior high. I didn't go in and lift any books. I'm not ready for that yet. But I did spend a long time hanging around, watching.

Schools here are so weird. There's not one or two main buildings that you go into and then walk interior halls to get to different classrooms. There's a whole bunch of buildings, and the halls are sidewalks. Even the lockers are outside! Maybe that's because they don't get snow here. Or much rain? (I hope.) But it doesn't seem very safe. Anyone (me or, say, your friendly neighborhood pervert) can just walk right onto the school premises. Sure, there's a fence, but it's wide open in front, and there are gaps all around that you can easily squeeze through. And the fence is just chain-link! Anyone can park on the street and watch. I wonder how many kids get abducted around here compared to, say, a place where they can lock kids in.

The flip side of that is that anyone can *leave,* too. I saw kids sneaking out through the back fence, kids smoking cigarettes behind the gym. . . . The setup is weird. It's like an invitation to be bad.

Oh! Something else weird about this school. Their flagpole has three flags: the American flag on top, the California flag in the middle, and underneath that a flag with a giant bullfrog on it. No kidding! This school's mascot is a *bullfrog.* Who wants to go to a school where perverts can abduct you and your mascot is a bullfrog?

Not me.

Next day (October 26^(th))

I went back to the overpass last night, and as I was pulling my sleeping bag out of my backpack, Charlene started giving me the third degree about where I'd been. When I didn't give much of an answer, she said, "You think you're better than us, is that it? Shoulda known when I seen your fancy beddin'." She sneered. "But you're back again,

ain'tcha? Here you are, back again." She hiked her blanket up over her shoulder and turned away from me, half singing, "You can check out any time you like, but you can never leave. . . ."

I didn't like the way that sounded.

I didn't like it at all.

The rest of them, though, thought it was hilarious.

7:30 p.m. Holed up in a McDonald's

I wandered back over to that school today. Just sat in the tall grass and watched. I don't know why I did it. Pretty lame, I guess.

It may only be a junior high, but kids seem a lot older than they did in elementary school. A lot more intimidating. (I wouldn't have thought that was possible, but it's true.) They dress a lot tougher, they *act* a lot tougher. Plus, the school itself looks sort of somber (except for the silly bullfrog flag). There's no playground equipment. No swings, no slides, no jungle gyms, no four-square courts . . . They do have basketball hoops and a couple of walls for handball, but I didn't see anyone using them. I guess kids think it's cooler to hang with their friends and act tough.

I hiked around town afterward, looking for a better place to crash tonight. There's an enclosed mall with bushes all around it, but the police station is real close by and cop cars seemed to be everywhere. And it's getting dark so early now. My safe zone (the time between school letting out and nightfall) is so short. I'll try again tomorrow, but tonight I'll have to go back to the overpass.

Wednesday the 27th

I walked from one end of this town to the other. It's actually a very boring, generic-looking town. Most of the buildings are one- or two-story stucco or block. Not a lot of trees (mostly scraggly pines that are tilted from standing in the wind). No parks or fountains or green spaces. Just fields and roads and stores.

Before I tell you the big thing that happened today, let me tell you about some of the places I discovered:

Place of interest #1: Cece's Thrift Store. It was full of total junk, but what made it sort of interesting was Cece, the woman who runs it. Picture piles of scarves and dangly bracelets on a homeless person. That's what she looks like! She's totally weathered and tough but dresses like a genie. I'd taken all of three steps inside the store when she growled, "Don't even think you can shoplift from me."

"Huh?" I said, because I couldn't believe anyone would have the guts to be that direct.

"You heard me," she said. But then she added, "Now if you want to barter, that's another story." She nodded at my backpack. "Whatcha haulin'?"

"Uh, nothing," I told her.

She snorted. "Then you won't mind leavin' it here."

"Huh?" I said again.

"Leave your overstuffed sack of nothing here." She pointed to a sign that read:

CHECK BAGS, BACKPACKS,
AND OVERSIZE PURSES AT THE COUNTER

"You know what?" I said. "I'll just come back later."

She laughed out loud, jangled a wave, and turned her back.

Place of interest #2: The library. It's okay. Almost medium-size. But I've never met a meaner children's librarian. I didn't give her a chance to snap at me, but the way she treated some of the other kids? Bite their heads off, why don't you? Never seen anything like it in a librarian.

So I borrowed a paperback (uh, that's *gypsy* borrowing). I was trying to avoid the security guard by sneaking out the back door, but instead I ran into a *real* cop. My heart about exploded, but he didn't pay any attention to me. He was on his way to City Hall, which is right next door to the library (and, it turns out, right up the street from the police station).

Place of interest #3 (and this is the REAL place of interest): A soup kitchen! I saw a group of bums sprawled on the grass in front of a gray wooden building and thought, What's this? Why are these guys lounging on a lawn right across from the courthouse? (Which, by the way, is on the *other* side of the police station, which is why bums hanging around surprised me.)

But then I saw *Charlene* coming down the building's ramp. It took me a minute to get over seeing her someplace besides the overpass, but then I noticed that she had *food*. A sandwich, a juice box, a bag of chips . . . shelter-style food.

I crossed the street and ran up to her, saying, "Charlene, wait up!"

When she saw it was me, she frowned. "What do you want?"

"Can you get me a sandwich, too?"

She snorted. "Go get your own!"

I let her walk away a few steps but then caught up to her. "Why didn't you tell me there was a soup kitchen?"

She did a mock inspection of her food, saying, "Soup? Do you see any soup? I don't see any soup."

"You know what I mean!" I whispered. "Why didn't you tell me?"

She smirked. "And ruin your healthy diet of pesticides?" Then she laughed and walked away.

I was so steamed I almost shouted, You heartless loser! We may sleep under the same bridge, but I will never be like you! I'm going to make something of myself! I'm going to do good in this world, and be good to this world, and I swear I will never, *ever* be like you.

I didn't say it, though. I kept it all inside. Steaming, hot and angry inside.

I found the soup kitchen.

I got my sandwich and juice.

I walked to the outskirts of town, where I sat on the bank of a broccoli field and thought. And thought. And thought. And this is what I've decided:

I am *not* going back to the overpass.

I *am* going to make a home for myself. I've done enough spinning my wheels. It's time to figure out a way to *do* it.

I *am* going to teach myself math and science and history, and maybe even art or music.

I *am* going to do good and be good, and someday, someway, I *will* become a veterinarian.

I swear on my mother's grave, I will.

FORGED

What's left to take from the broken?
Or . . . what can the broken repair!
I am the steel
Life is the flame
Time is the endless hammer clanging

What's to become of me now?
Or . . . what shall I now become!
I am the steel
Life is the flame
Time is the endless hammer clanging

What final blow will break me?
Or . . . what will my new form defeat!
I am the steel
Life is the flame
Time is the endless hammer clanging

November 1st

I have been a busy, busy bee! No time for journaling, I've been building a house! I'm not kidding! I am so excited I can hardly stand it!!!

First I found a really great place to set up camp. It's a soft, sandy area with lots of shrubs and tall grasses, and it's near a wide, dried-up riverbed. There's not one single drop of water anywhere around here, and from the way things are growing in the riverbed, I think it must have been ages and ages since water flowed through it. The good thing is that I'm isolated but not too far from the soup kitchen.

Next I found a big cardboard box. Don't laugh. Cardboard works great for protection from wind, sun, and cold. Street people use cardboard all the time, and bum alleys are like little cardboard cities. The houses in bum alleys are just shanties or lean-tos, though. They're nothing like my house! Mine is deluxe! It's a big, thick, supersturdy refrigerator box that I found behind an appliance store. I ripped off the tape and took out the big staples, collapsed it, and hauled it clear out here to the riverbed. (It was a small miracle that no cops stopped me, but they didn't.)

That took me all day. Then for the past few days I've been busy building! I leveled the ground (with a flat rock, my hands, and my feet), then went back to town and got some construction supplies (like packing tape and Hefty sacks).

On my building site I laid down a Hefty sack (to keep moisture from the ground from seeping into the cardboard), reassembled the box, and put it on top of the Hefty sack. Then I covered the top of the box with two Hefty sacks and camouflaged the whole thing with tumbleweeds.

I've gone back to town a couple of times to get supplies. Cans of food, toilet paper, bottled water, fresh batteries for my flashlight . . . and right now I'm snuggled up in my sleeping bag, warm and cozy, looking around at this place, and I can't believe it. I've got a house!

A home!

This is heaven!

I'VE GOT MY VERY OWN HOME!

November 3rd

I took the day off yesterday and read my library book. It was pretty good until the end, which just sort of fizzled. But it was fun to hang around my own house and read! It does get pretty warm in here during the day, but at night it's perfect.

One day off was enough, though. I wanted to get going on learning math and science so I can become a veterinarian! So early this morning I went back to that junior high school, and when kids started arriving, I walked onto the school grounds like I belonged and asked some boy where the science teacher's room was.

"Mr. Pence?" He pointed. "Right over there."

So I went over to Mr. Pence's room. No other kids were in the classroom yet, but there was a man setting up microscopes on a long table.

Mr. Pence, I presume!

He barely noticed me. Didn't say good morning or even nod, so neither did I.

I scanned the room quick. There was a big stack of books on a back counter, so I sidled up to them, slid one off, and slinked out the back door.

It was definitely worth the risk. You should see this book! It's amazing. I read a section about how eyes work. It's fascinating! It also explained that dogs don't just see in black and white (something I've always thought, but people told me I was wrong). Dogs have blue and green receptors in their eyes (just like humans). The only thing we have that they don't is the red photoreceptor (which means that they can't see red, and may see orange and yellow as gray).

So it's been a really great day, but now I've got to get over to the soup kitchen before they close. I'm hungry!

7:15 p.m.

A little information about the soup kitchen:

It's run by priests and nuns, and the nice thing about that is, they don't ask any questions. You just get your food and go. I've been going in on the heels of somebody I pretend is my parent, but it doesn't seem to matter. The people who work there don't really seem to *see* you, which is perfect for me.

It's funny to hear priests and nuns argue with each other. It's just not something you expect, but these do it a lot, and because of that I've picked up some of their names:

There's Brother Phil, who's paunchy and balding and bossy and doesn't seem to like anybody. Then there's Sister Mary Margaret, who is very nice, and Sister Josephine, who's a hunched-over battle-ax! You wouldn't believe her. She's old and crabby and slams her cane around whenever someone (especially Brother Phil) makes her mad.

So from overhearing them talk and argue, I've pieced together that they're from St. Mary's Church (which is a few blocks away from the soup kitchen), *and* today I overheard Sister Mary Margaret talking to Josephine about the church's Thanksgiving food drive. It went like this:

> *Mary Margaret:* I'm worried. Last year at this time
> we had so much more!
> *Josephine (muttering):* You worry every year, Sister.
> *Mary Margaret:* But this year feels different!
> This year—
> *Josephine (still muttering):* This year'll be just like every
> year. The foyer'll fill up. The families will be fed.
> *Mary Margaret:* But what if—
> *Josephine (slamming down her cane, shouting):*
> Sister! It's only the third of November! Give it time!

See? Isn't that very un-nunlike? They're always like that. It busts me up.

Next morning

I woke up with a brilliant idea!

If St. Mary's Church is having a food drive, maybe I can help myself to some of it when no one's looking! I'll be a gypsy squirrel, collecting cans for the winter!

It sounded like they're just having people drop off stuff in the church foyer. . . .

I'm going to go check it out!

12:30 p.m.

I went to the church. Didn't see any food at all. I didn't stay very long because I had a weird feeling being there. I'll check better later.

There's a school next door to the church. Kids in uniforms were playing on the blacktop. Squealing, laughing, shouting. I never really listened to the sound of a playground before. It sounds happy. Lively. Exciting.

I don't remember it that way.

I just remember the fear.

Wait. Maybe way early on it was more excitement than fear, but after we started moving around so much . . . and then after Mom died . . . and after the Fisks . . . fear is what I remember most.

Right now I'm back at Bullfrog Junior High. (That's not the real name of the school, but it should be.) I don't know why I came, really. I wasn't planning to get myself a math book or anything. I've barely started on the science.

I wound up sitting in the weeds behind the back fence, and I've been watching the girls' PE classes play softball. Softball in November, can you imagine? And you know what else is amazing? None of the girls have acted like sissies. Some of them aren't very good, but they all really try. And everybody chatters and shouts and cheers when their team does something good. It's like they're playing some big game, only it's just PE.

I used to hate PE at school. Two times a week (oh, that'll get you in shape!), lame games (you call "duck-duck-goose" PE?), choosing up sides (took up half the class and made you feel rotten for the rest of the day), and no action (like anyone's going to pass the ball to a kid they don't know or like?).

Yeah, I used to hate PE, but *this* kind of PE looks like it could almost be fun. So I'm sitting here wondering what it would be like to be on a real team. To have people rooting for you . . . to feel like you were part of something . . . electric.

6:30 p.m.

I didn't see Charlene at the soup kitchen this afternoon, but I saw Martin, which was much worse. His body's so covered in snakes that I think he's *become* a snake. Maybe he doesn't have fangs (his teeth are all rotten), but he sure seems to slither around. And you know how a snake's tongue flicks in and out? Martin *looks* at things like that. He flicks looks here and there, and I can tell he's watching, thinking, scheming. It scares me because whenever I catch him flicking looks my way, I get the feeling that he's coiled up tight, waiting for the right opportunity to strike.

Walking home tonight, I really watched my back.

No one would ever hear me scream out here.

No one would know if I went missing.

Friday, November 5th

I checked out St. Mary's Church again. No boxes or bags of food in sight. I even wandered *into* the church and looked around from the safety of a shadowy back pew.

There's something spooky about churches like St. Mary's. Any little noise echoes off the stained-glass windows and seems to amplify before it dies out. Voices carry. Everything seems close, even when it's far away.

There was nobody inside the church besides me, but there *was* a strange sound. I couldn't figure out where it was coming from or how far away it was, but the longer I sat in that shadowy back pew, the more it sounded like it was someone *gnawing* on something.

Then a priest came into the church, looked around, and whispered, "Gregory?" He whistled softly. "Gregory? Here, boy. Come along, lad!" He had some sort of accent. Irish, I think.

I heard Gregory pad through the church, then saw him pass by the aisle. He was the cutest wirehaired terrier, and he was carrying a *carrot* in his mouth.

I almost burst out laughing. And I wanted so badly to jump and say, "Oh! Can I say hi to your dog?" But I just watched him join the priest and disappear through a side door.

I stayed in the church a little while longer, but I wasn't thinking about getting my hands on food-drive donations. I was thinking about getting my hands on a dog. Not Gregory. I would never steal somebody else's dog! What I mean is a dog from the pound. Or a stray. Or a poor, neglected, abused, chained-up dog.

Maybe it's finally time to get one.

My heart's beating fast just thinking about it!

And you know what? I *need* a dog. Not just so I won't be so alone, but for the protection. Dogs are great at defending their territory.

They also know how to scare off snakes.

7:00 p.m.

I am so mad! The pound won't let a kid have a dog unless a parent signs for it. Can you believe that? They'd rather "destroy" (their way of sugarcoating *kill*) a dog than let a kid have it! I hate adults! I hate them, I hate them, I hate them!

8:15 p.m.

The pound is like death row for dogs, only the dogs haven't done anything wrong! (Except maybe pee on some old bat's posies . . .) I'd rescue them all if I could.

Poor sweet things.

Saturday the 6th

I've been trying to read my science book, but some of it isn't making sense and my mind keeps drifting. I keep picturing dogs getting gassed. And every time I hear a sound outside, I think it's Martin. He was slithering around the soup kitchen again today, and after I left, I caught him following me. I didn't let on. Instead, I led him to the mall, then ditched him. It was easy, but I don't like having to do it.

And now I'm *really* thinking that I need some way to protect myself.

One of those softball bats I saw at the junior high would be good.

A nice, heavy metal one.

9:30 p.m.

There's a whole pack of coyotes howling. It's so loud I swear they're right outside my house! I keep telling myself: They're dogs, they're dogs, they're dogs! But I'm still scared. Coyotes kill cats and rabbits and other *dogs*. What if they're so hungry they'll kill *me*?

How ironic would that be?

Holly Janquell, aspiring veterinarian, killed and consumed by dogs.

If I live through the night, I'm gathering rocks.

And I'm getting my hands on a baseball bat!

November 7th

It's Sunday, so I couldn't get my hands on a baseball bat, but better yet, I have made a deadly spear! I scored a broom handle from a trash bin outside the mall (the threads are messed up, but other than that it's perfect), and I traded a sack of sweaters I scored at the Salvation Army for a knife at Cece's Thrift Store. (The Salvation Army is real near the soup kitchen, and they were having a *warmth* drive today. The whole front porch was covered with sacks of clothes, and the woman in charge was so busy yakking with someone else that she didn't notice me waltz off with one. I picked out a change of clothes for me, then traded the rest for a knife.)

This is no little whittling blade, either. It's wicked! Thick and jagged and long. Cece was cool about it, too. No questions, no raised eyebrows. She just dug through the sack of clothes and said, "Fair trade. It's yours."

I've duct-taped the knife to the broom handle, and now I have a spear that could bring down a bear!

I'm feeling much, much better.

9:15 p.m.

I overheard a little of the sermon at St. Mary's when I slipped inside the church this morning to check the foyer for food. (There was nothing.) The priest with the Irish accent was saying how the whole month of November should be devoted to giving and thanking.

I split after about thirty seconds.

Like I need to hear that garbage?

But tonight it's really cold out, and it's making me remember past Novembers. Especially the one when I didn't have a down sleeping bag and a heavy jacket to keep me warm; when there was snow on the ground and no place to sleep and no refrigerator box to keep out the wind. That was a November when I really *couldn't* imagine a single, solitary thing to be thankful for.

So I'm realizing that this year *is* different. There have been better Novembers, sure, but this year I *am* doing okay. Even having no family at Thanksgiving doesn't really bother me. I miss my mom, but it's not like I ever had a huge family to share a turkey feast with.

Actually, I've never even had a turkey feast.

Ever.

Even in the days before we were on the streets, my mom used to get two boxes of KFC—chicken, mashed potatoes, and biscuits—and that's what we'd have for Thanksgiving dinner.

I remember asking her once when we were sitting down to KFC, "Can we please, please, *please* roast a turkey next year?"

"Oh, baby," she said. "You have no idea what you're *not* missing. Turkey's a *tough* bird. A tough, disgusting, wattley bird that, honestly, no one *really* wants to eat."

213

"But—" I said, but she cut me off.

"Don't let the tradition of turkey fool you, baby. Turkey is all that was available to the Pilgrims at the time." She flicked out a napkin and said, "Our founding fathers didn't have KFC at their disposal or you can bet your bottom dollar they'd have ordered a bucket of Extra Crispy instead of roasting an ornery, oversize rooster!"

I still felt like I was missing out, so I asked, "But can't we try it? Just once?"

She sighed and rolled her eyes. "Baby, it's just you and me! Do you have any idea what goes into roasting a turkey? First you've got to cook it for five, maybe eight hours—basting it the whole while—and when the dark meat's finally cooked, the white meat's so dry it needs to be slathered in gravy and cranberries just so you can swallow it. Believe me. You'd be *very* disappointed." She bit into a KFC drumstick and said, "Now *this* is delicious. It's moist and crispy and tasty. *This* is what a turkey *dreams* of bein'." She wagged the drumstick at me and said, "Eat up, baby. Eat up! This is *our* tradition, and believe me, it's way better than the old tradition!"

The funny thing is, though, every Thanksgiving she'd open a big can of spiced peaches and a small can of cranberry sauce to go with the KFC. And she'd get this faraway look in her eye when she ate them.

Like she was remembering something.

Maybe a dream.

Monday, November 8th

There were sacks of food in the church foyer today! I grabbed one that was full of cans and split before anyone saw.

Score!

I've now got an amazing stash of spaghetti, pineapple, beans, stew, tuna, Spam, tamales, nuts . . . I am set for weeks!

But best of all, in the middle of the sack, I found a can of cranberry sauce and another of spiced peaches!

Spiced peaches!

My mouth is watering just thinking about them!

I'm saving them for Thanksgiving, though.

And sometime between now and then I'm tracking down a KFC.

Tuesday the 9th

I saw Gregory today. That priest with the Irish accent was tossing a carrot for him like a stick. It was so funny!

I was planning to get my hands on a math book or maybe a language book (one of those with lots of short stories in them—I like those), but on my way over to the junior high it began to drizzle and I started worrying about my house, so I came home. I'm glad I did, too, because there were puddles forming around the base of it. I think it was runoff from the roof, which was kind of surprising (and scary) because it didn't rain very hard at all.

I was wishing for a shovel to dig a trench to divert the water, but the ground is really sandy and I was able to scrape out a pretty good gully with a can. (I used beans, not peaches!)

It took a while to do, and I was pretty wet and dirty by the time I was through, so I almost didn't go out to the soup kitchen (because I have plenty of food here), but that would have been lazy of me.

The soup kitchen turned out to be pretty entertaining because I got to hear the tail end of a "Brother and Sister" shouting match:

> *Brother Phil:* Why do I always have to do it?
> You do it!
> *Sister Josephine (pointing her cane at him):*
> Because it's your job to do it!
> *Phil:* Why's it my job? Who says it's my job?
> *Josephine:* Father says!
> *Phil (storming off):* Well, it's not fair!
> *Josephine (muttering):* Neither is having to work
> with you!

I have no idea what they were arguing about, but it made me laugh. These are grown-up people, and they're arguing like little kids. Like a real brother and sister.

You know what? If I had a brother or sister, I would just refuse to fight. What could possibly be worth fighting over? If you've got family, you've got everything.

Wednesday, 2:15 p.m.

I tried reading my science book today, but my mind kept drifting again. It's making me mad. I'm supposed to be teaching myself the things I'll need to become a veterinarian, but I've had this science book for a week and haven't finished one chapter. Who am I fooling? What kind of ridiculous "plan" is this?

I keep thinking about family, too. Wishing for family. Remembering all the times I sabotaged my chances of being part of someone else's family.

I wish I could go back. I wish I had taken a chance on someone who was willing to take a chance on me.

I just wasn't ready then.

And now it's too late.

3:30 p.m.

I've got to stop thinking about this and look at the bright side. I mean, come on! I've got it made here! I'm not hungry. I'm not cold. I have my own place with no one telling me what to do.

Why am I seeing the things I don't have again instead of the things I do?

I think I'll go for a walk.

Clear my head.

Find something else to think about.

Thursday

There was a girl my age serving food at the soup kitchen this afternoon.

I didn't like it.

I felt embarrassed.

Why is she working there?

Is she a nun in training?

A goody-two-shoes?

She didn't look like it.

She looked a lot like . . . me.

Thursday night

I went for a long walk up the riverbank. The scenery's pretty much the same as far as you can see. Scrubby trees, tumbleweeds, tall grass, sandy soil . . . It was starting to get dark, and I was just thinking what a boring waste of time the walk had been when I stubbed my toe on a horseshoe.

A horseshoe!

And while I was pulling it out of the sand, I unearthed another one, buried right beside it.

They made a wonderful sound when I clinked the sand off of them. A Wild West sound. A strike-it-rich sound.

They're making me feel very lucky.

Friday, November 12th

That girl was at the soup kitchen again today. She started to ask me something, but I tore out of there before she could. The last thing I need is some nosy nun-in-training quizzing me up about stuff that's none of her business.

The good news is that Martin wasn't hanging around today. Neither was Charlene. Maybe they've moved on. Or been arrested.

One can always hope.

Sunday

The sky looks so heavy today. Dark and gloomy and *angry*. It's really humid inside my house. I've got the door propped open, but it's not helping much. I'm thinking I should have used tarps to protect my house instead of Hefty sacks. Tarps are way thicker.

I just looked up at the sky again. It's huge. All that water building up, waiting to rain down. Why didn't I ever get an umbrella? I could really use an umbrella.

Maybe I can trade in the horseshoes.

2:00 p.m.

I AM SO MAD!!!!!!!! All this time I was worried about Martin, and I should have been worried about that stupid nun-in-training! I came back from a bad encounter with Cece only to find that stupid girl ransacking my house! I jabbed my spear at her and you should have seen her eyes pop. She was shaking in her shoes because she knew I was ready to run her through! Who does she think she is? THIS IS MY HOUSE!

But then her quivery voice said, "Don't kill me, Holly! I'm sorry!"

All I could hear was my name, echoing inside my head.

How did she know my name?

"Holly, please," she said, holding my sleeping bag in front of her. "Just put down the knife. I'm not here to steal anything."

I jabbed my spear in closer, even though there was no way I was going to slice up my sleeping bag. "Who sent you?" I asked through my teeth. Fear and anger and betrayal were all combusting inside me. How *dare* she?

"Nobody sent me!" she quivered. "Nobody!"

I didn't believe her. Not for a second. "It was those nuns, wasn't it? Those stupid nosy nuns. How'd they find out who I was? Have they been—"

"No!" she said. "Your name's in your jacket! And I'm only here because I thought you might have Father Mayhew's goblets and cross."

"Goblets and cross? What goblets and cross?"

"He thought *I* took them, and I saw you in church the other day, and when you came through the food line, I heard something clinking in your backpack and I thought—"

"Well, you thought wrong!" I shouted, jabbing the spear at her again. Then I really let her have it. "You thought breaking into a cardboard box wouldn't be the same thing as breaking into someone's home, didn't you! You thought tearing through someone's bags of stuff wouldn't be the same as tearing through someone's kitchen or closet, didn't you? You probably live in some cushy little house and sleep in some cushy little bed and have someone put a warm meal in front of your spoiled little face every night!"

"You're wrong!" she shouted back. "I live in a seniors-only apartment with my grandmother where kids aren't even allowed! I have to sneak up the fire escape so no one sees me! Everything I own fits into my grandmother's bottom drawer!"

"Oh, poor you," I said, but I was thinking, Man! This girl knows how to come up with a lie *quick.*

Then she said, "So maybe I don't live in a box, but there's no way I've got it *cushy.*" She frowned and added, "And I am sorry. I really am. My friends and I followed you out here on Friday because we . . ."

I don't even know what the end of the sentence was. All I heard was "my friends and I." It was like a slug to the stomach. I staggered backward and sat on the riverbank. I couldn't seem to catch my breath.

Her *friends*? How many people knew? How long would it be before some stupid social worker got sent to "rescue" me?

My beautiful house. My first real home. It was over. I was going to have to move.

She caught me crying, which made me madder than ever. "This place was perfect!" I sobbed. "Why couldn't you just have left me alone!"

"We won't tell, I promise!"

I snorted and slapped away tears. "Oh, sure. Right. Like I believe that!"

She sat next to me and said, "But why are you living down here?"

I jumped up and shouted, "Because I'm sick of people treating me like dirt! Because I don't want some foster-home jerk locking me in a closet or Sani-Flushing me ever again!" Her eyes were really popping now, so I snapped, "And why are you working at the soup kitchen? You some sort of nun-in-training?"

She blinked at me, then laughed really hard. "A nun-in-training?

No! I'm working off detention for school. They gave me twenty hours for 'using and abusing the school's PA system.' " She grinned at me. "Among other things."

Among other things? I wanted to laugh, but I stopped myself. I wanted to hate her, but somehow I couldn't.

Twenty hours of detention?

The most I'd ever gotten was two!

I was dying to ask, *How* did you use and abuse the school's PA system? What school? Do you go to that bullfrog school? What's it like? Twenty hours? Wow! But I stopped myself in the nick of time. "Look," I growled at her. "This place took me a long time to build and I don't feel like moving." I grabbed my spear again. "So if you or one of your little friends decide to rat on me . . ."

"We won't!" she said. "Trust me, we won't!"

I snorted. "Trust you? *Trust* you? What kind of idiot do you think I am?"

"Well, I trusted you!" she said. "I told you all sorts of top-secret stuff!"

I sneered at her. "Shows how bright *you* are . . ." Then I shrugged and said, "So if you don't want me spillin' your secret, don't spill mine."

The funny thing is, she thought that was a fair bargain, even though her secret seems worthless compared to mine. I don't even know where she lives or what her name is or anything. But if she's worried about me ratting her off, fine. I'll use it.

I sure hope she keeps her mouth shut because I can't exactly move now. I'm sure it's going to rain any minute.

Besides, I don't *want* to move.

This is my home.

Monday the 15th

No cops showed up last night, but I'm kicking myself for not following *her* home yesterday. If I knew where she lived, then I'd really
have something to hold over her head.

Hmm. I wonder how many "seniors-only" apartments this town has.

And she mentioned a fire escape.

Maybe I *can* track her down. . . .

I've also got to track down a shovel. It rained a little last night, and
although it didn't unload like I thought it might, the sky's still heavy
and angry-looking, and it's going to. Soon.

I tried trenching a little deeper with a can, but even with the soil
moist, it's slow and hard.

Maybe I could score a shovel from someone's backyard. Or, hey!
How about from a gardener's truck. Or a road-repair truck! Yeah! I
bet there are hundreds of shovels out there just waiting to come home
with me.

I should have thought of this days ago. . . .

Almost 4 p.m.

I am chock-full of new information!

Here's what I found out today:

There are four senior buildings in town, but only one has fire escape
stairs. (I called them all from a pay phone, and the other three places
said, "They're not necessary here. We're only a single-story facility.")

223

So now I know where she lives *and* . . .

I also know she goes to the bullfrog school! I wandered over there because it's not far from the seniors building, and there was some big-deal girls' softball game going on. The whole school was out cheering and whistling. It was an intense game. The coaches actually got into a fight! No fists flew, but there was a lot of shouting, and some big guy had to step in to break it up.

And it turns out the girl played catcher! I didn't recognize her at first because of all the equipment she was wearing, but when she flipped off her catcher's mask to go after a ball, I recognized her!

Guess what else? When she caught the ball, the pitcher shouted, "Way to go, Sammie!"

So I also know her name!

If she wants to cause me trouble, man, I am ready to rumble!

I am also ready for rain (I hope). I snagged a gardener's shovel off his trailer and used it to dig a nice wide trench clear around the house.

I still wish I had an umbrella.

I wonder if I can make it to the soup kitchen before it starts to rain. . . .

6:20 p.m.

I am an idiot! Why did I have to try to make it to the soup kitchen? I should have just eaten at home! I was planning to tell that Sammie girl that I knew all about where she lived and that she'd better not go back on her word, but halfway to the soup kitchen the sky opened up and tried to DROWN me. I could not believe how fast and furious that water fell.

I shouldn't even have gone inside the soup kitchen, but I did. And by then I was hoping that that Sammie girl *wasn't* there, but she was.

"Are you all right?" she asked.

"Yeah," I growled.

"I . . . I could get you some dry clothes," she whispered.

"Don't even!" I told her. "I'm fine. It's just water." Then I split.

My hair's still soaked, and my shoes are going to take forever to dry out. But I've stripped out of everything and I'm in dry clothes, in my sleeping bag. I'm still shivering, but I can feel myself warming up.

The rain's pounding on the roof. It's so loud, even through the tumbleweeds. But the good news is, the house is holding up. If it can make it through this downpour, it can make it though anything!

2:30 a.m.

It's still pouring. One wall of my house is soaked and the floor below it is starting to get wet.

I don't want to go outside and trench.

I don't want to get drenched again.

But I don't want to lose my house.

Please stop raining. Please, please, please stop raining!

225

4:50 a.m.

It's *still* raining. I finally went out and trenched. It was brutal. Windy. Cold. I could barely see what I was doing.

I tried putting up an extra Hefty sack, but it just blew away. I'm having real trouble warming up now. I'm cold down to my bones.

I wish I had put more Hefty sacks under the house. If my sleeping bag gets wet, I'm doomed.

I do think the trenching helped.

And at least the roof's not leaking.

5:05 a.m.

Here's a cheery thought:

The roof on the *Titanic* didn't leak, either.

5:25

I am still so cold.

Half the floor is soaked.

I wish I knew which apartment that Sammie girl lived in.

I wonder if she'd let me in if I showed up at her door. . . .

Next day, 2:45 p.m.

Things are bad. The house is soggy in so many places. I've never thought of water as evil before, but right now I do. It stopped raining a few hours ago, so I'm airing out my wet clothes and the sleeping bag, but I don't think the house will dry today unless it gets some direct sun, and that's not looking too likely. It's still overcast. I don't think I can make it through another night like last night.

Midnight

I don't even know if I can talk about this.

I'm shaky and scared.

And I'm so tired.

So, *so* tired.

But I can't sleep. I feel like I'll never be able to sleep again.

So I'm going to write. . . .

Where to start.

I guess with Martin.

I ran into town to get more Hefty sacks. I actually *paid* for them. I was in a hurry, and I wanted to save my house more than I wanted to save what little money I had left.

Maybe I was so preoccupied with getting back to my poor house that I didn't notice Martin following me. And when I saw him come out of the bushes, I should have run, but I didn't. I picked up my spear and shouted, "Get out of here, you creep!"

He sneered.

And laughed.

And moved closer.

"Get back!" I shouted.

He kept coming, and the look on his face made my stomach turn. Mr. Fisk flashed through my mind, and I couldn't help shaking.

"Nice place," he said, still sneering. "Nice and secluded."

That's when I noticed he was going toward the shovel. He was planning to use it to block my spear.

I had to move or lose.

227

Up from somewhere deep and dark, an awful noise came out of me. And when I charged, the memory of Mr. Fisk propelled me forward with a fury that I didn't even know I still had inside.

"LEAVE . . . ME . . . ALONE!" I shouted, but in an instant he'd twisted the spear out of my hands and thrown it aside, leaving me stunned and off balance.

He grabbed me, so I kicked him in the shin as hard as I could, which made him so mad he hurled me against some bushes.

"No!" I cried, scrambling to get on my feet as he came at me. I tried desperately to get away, but he caught me and held me, two wrists in one hand.

There was no mercy in him, I could see it.

There was no hope for me, I could feel it.

He was so much stronger than I was.

So much crueler.

Still, I squirmed and kicked frantically. I was so mad. So burning-up mad. How could he overpower me so easily? It was unfair! So maddeningly unfair.

All my struggling just made him laugh harder, and I could feel myself getting weaker. And inside I was panicking because I knew there was no way I could win.

Forget win. There was no way I could even get away.

Then all of a sudden it was like a bolt of lightning hit him. He made a bloodcurdling scream and just let go.

In the blink of an eye that Sammie girl was standing beside me, pointing the metal tip of the biggest, blackest umbrella I have ever seen right at Martin. "Get away from her," she yelled at him. "Get away from her or I'll run you through!"

"There's *two* of you brats?" he cried, holding his back where she'd rammed him.

"Yeah, there's two of us!" I shouted. "Now leave us alone!"

He started to retreat but then turned back and grabbed my sleeping bag. And while we were struggling with him over that, he tripped on the trench and lost his balance, falling back . . . back . . . back . . . and landing on my house.

"No!" I screamed as the box collapsed, folding in all around him.

I couldn't bear to look, so I turned away, then crumbled to the ground and started to cry.

My home. My dream. My life.

It was over.

Ruined.

Somehow Sammie chased Martin off, then sat next to me and put her arm around me. "I'm so sorry," she whispered. "I'm so, so sorry."

"What am I going to do?" I gasped. "What am I going to *do*?"

After a minute she took my hand and pulled me to my feet. "You're going to come with me," she said. "I have an idea."

I guess I could have refused to go with her, but I didn't. I followed her, and inside I felt strangely relieved.

Relieved to actually believe I could trust her.

We didn't say much to each other as we walked into town. She seemed to be thinking really hard about something, and frankly, I was too exhausted to talk.

I was surprised when we passed by her apartment building, because I'd thought that's where we were going. I almost said something about knowing she lived there, but I didn't. I just followed her as she jaywalked across the street and led me to a *dog* kennel.

At least that's what I thought it was at first. It was really a dog-grooming shop with an apartment upstairs, and after a few minutes of Sammie leaning on the buzzer, a wiry woman answered the door. She was wearing a bathrobe and slippers.

In a daze I followed them to the upstairs apartment. Another woman was doing dishes at the sink. Who were these people? Why had Sammie brought me here? Wouldn't they just call social services?

Sammie introduced us. The wiry one was Vera, the younger one was Meg.

Sammie explained that I'd had a really bad time in foster homes. She told them that I'd been living down by the riverbed. She told them about my refrigerator box. Her words became a blur of sound. I just sat there scared and shaky.

The women didn't say much, but the faces they pulled? No one had to spell it out: They didn't want anything to do with me.

Then Meg started pacing around, talking about friends of theirs who have foster children. "They're saints!" she said. "Their house is spotless and their children are happy!"

Sammie jumped up and said, "Maybe it's like dog kennels. You know, some of them are good and clean and others, well, dogs come out with kennel cough and fleas, smelling like pee!"

We all stared at her.

She shrugged and said, "Maybe Holly just happened to get stuck in some rotten, uh, kennels."

Meg and Vera seemed to think this was an extreme comparison, but there was something about it that I really liked. And I didn't want to even go there, but I couldn't help really liking *her.*

But then the older one (Vera) asked me what happened to my parents and how old I was, so I did what I always do:

I lied.

I told them that I didn't even remember my parents and that I was fifteen.

Why bother with the truth? I could tell that they were trying to figure out how to avoid having me stay with them, even for one night. No sense getting into the truth. No sense at all.

But Vera leveled a look at me and said, "The truth, dear. If we're going to talk about this, you need to tell us the truth."

It was the way she said it, I think. So calm and wise and *kind.*

And then I remembered what I'd thought after I'd escaped Walt and Valerie:

I should have wagged.

I should have begged.

I should have *tried.*

My chin started quivering, and before I knew what I was saying, I blurted, "I'm only twelve!" Then I started sobbing.

When my mom died, I felt like I was lost in a giant black forest. I'd never cried so hard in my life. I don't think there's a pain in this world as awful as that one. Still, I was crying like I had that day. After all I'd been through to break free, to be free, to make it on my own, I'd still failed.

"Please," I choked out. "I don't know who to turn to. I need someone I can trust. Please don't call social services. Just let me stay here for one night." My throat ached from being pinched so tight, but I whispered it again, anyway. "I'm not a bad person. I've just been through some really bad times."

Through a blur of tears, I saw a tiny poodle jump into my lap. It was soft and light and so sweet, stretching up to lick tears from my cheeks, my eyes, my nose.

My chin quivered terribly as I smiled at it and whispered, "Hi there."

"That's Lucy," Vera said. "Or Miss Lucille, when she's being naughty."

I wrapped her in my arms and whispered, "Hi, Lucy. Thank you."

Lucy wagged her little tail and licked some more tears from my cheek, which made me laugh and cry at the same time.

Vera and Meg excused themselves to have a private meeting in a back room, and when they returned they told me I could stay the night. They also promised that they wouldn't call social services behind my back, and said that we would talk more in the morning.

I hope I can trust them, but if not I've already decided I'm going to run.

Pouring rain or not, I'll run.

For tonight, though, I'm warm and safe, in my own little room, in my own little bed. There are patchwork quilts hanging on the walls, and one on the bed. They give the room such a cozy feeling, but best of all, Lucy's asleep beside me in bed.

She is so sweet.

So, so sweet.

And I am so, so tired. . . .

Sunday, November 21st

I can't believe I've been here five days already. The time has gone by so fast! There's so much to write about, but I'll start with Meg and Vera. (Meg is Vera's daughter, by the way.) They seem so ordinary, but they're not. They have this quiet strength about them, which I really like. They work hard, but they don't complain, and they may have laid down some strict rules for me, but they're so kind about it that I don't mind following them.

I love the way they talk to dogs in the shop. "Come here, baby. That's my girl." "Uh-uh-uh, you rascal, none of that in here!" They wash and dry and shear and style dogs, and they treat every single one of them like a long-lost friend.

I love helping them in the shop, which they let me do after I get home from school.

That's right, *school.* Can you believe it? I'm already enrolled in the bullfrog school. It all happened so quick, and I was really nervous at first, but I have Sammy (that's how she spells it) in homeroom and she's been helping me a lot. She showed me around and introduced me to her friends, and they invited me to sit at their lunch table. I don't say much. I mostly just listen to them talk about softball, but I'm really grateful that they include me.

The schoolwork's kind of hard. Especially math. But Vera and Meg have promised to get me tutoring if I have trouble catching up. "You can do this, Holly," Meg told me. "And we're going to help you any way we can."

It's been funny to see the change in Meg. At first she was real wary. She was constantly watching me out of the corner of her eye.

234

I've been on my best behavior, but I think it's actually Lucy who's convinced her that I'm okay. Lucy follows me everywhere. She sits on the counter when I do the dishes, she sits in my lap as I do my homework, she sleeps on my bed and goes crazy when I get home from school. That dog is just a little bundle of waggy love.

So Meg's gone from being pretty suspicious of me to acting a little like Lucy. She hovers around me while I'm eating breakfast; she likes to dry the dishes while I'm washing them (even though they'd drip-dry just fine); and Friday when I jingled through the downstairs door, she called, "Holly's home!" across the shop to Vera, like they'd been waiting for me all day.

Do you know how nice that sounded?

"Holly's home!"

What musical, magical words.

Tuesday, November 23rd

This morning at breakfast Meg told me that they would fight anyone (like a social worker) who tries to take me from them. She leaned across the table and whispered, "This arrangement may not be legal yet, but we have a plan: If someone comes to take you away, you *run* away, and after they're gone, you come right back."

I laughed and said okay, because coming from an adult, it sounded crazy.

I also laughed because I liked the way it made me feel like it was *us* against them, instead of just *me* against them.

It's been a long time since I've felt that way.

A long, long time.

235

Tuesday, 4:30 p.m.

I overheard Meg talking on the phone to someone at social services. I don't understand why things have to be so complicated. Why does everything have to be so "official"? Why do courts have to be petitioned? Why do people who have never met me think they know what's best for me?

I'm afraid to let out this breath I've been holding.

I'm afraid that my bubble of hope will just collapse.

November 25th, Thanksgiving

I'm still here! And today's the day I get my wish for a big Thanksgiving feast. I should be feeling happy about it, but I'm actually a little sad.

I wish my mom could be here.

Meg asked me if I had any special wishes, and I'm afraid my eyes filled with tears when I asked for spiced peaches.

We started baking pies around seven this morning. It smells so good in the apartment. I don't think I've ever smelled anything like it. The turkey's been roasting for hours, so the air is a mixture of sizzling fat, salt, and sweet. It smells divine! (Lucy thinks so, too. The aroma's making her a little crazy. She's gotten quite a few "Miss Lucille . . . !" warnings from Vera and Meg for begging.)

It's been fun helping in the kitchen. I've never really done that before. Peeling, grating, measuring, mixing . . . I like it all, especially because Vera and Meg sing while they work. The songs they know are really old-fashioned, but I like them. They fill the air with joy.

We haven't been cooking for just the three of us, either. Sammy and her grandmother and her grandmother's boyfriend are also coming. It'll be a full house!

Thanksgiving, 9:00 p.m.

What an emotional night. Sammy's grandmother's boyfriend was just about to carve the turkey when Vera said, "Before we eat, I think we should take a moment and give thanks." Then she looked around the table and said, "Maybe we could each say a few words?"

Vera started, closing her eyes and putting her hands together and saying, "Dear Lord, I'm thankful for many things this day: for the food, for the company, but especially for the chance we've been given to open up our home to Holly."

Right away I got choked up. Then Meg went, saying, "Thank you, Lord, for all you've given us this year, but mostly, thank you for bringing Holly to us."

She started to add something else, but we were peeking at each other over our clasped hands, and both of us were watery-eyed, so she just smiled.

Next around the table was Sammy, and while I was trying to blink back my tears, she was sitting there like a deer caught in the headlights. I couldn't tell if her mind was a blank or if she was thinking a million miles an hour. But after a minute of everyone waiting she blurted out, "I'm thankful that's a real turkey and not a roasting chicken!"

I busted up. If I had been taking a drink, I would have sprayed it all over the table. That one sentence said a million things to me. And in that instant I knew we were going to have to compare notes about the Thanksgiving dinners we'd had in the past. I knew that I would tell her about wishing for a turkey and getting KFC. And I had the wonderful feeling that it wouldn't stop there, that little by little we would get to know each other better.

I do want to get to know her better.

And I want her to know the real me.

Still Thanksgiving, almost 10:00 p.m.

Meg peeked in my room when I was writing before. She was coming in to kiss me good night (which she does every night), but

238

when she saw the journal she stopped short. "You keep a journal?" she asked, and the odd thing is, she looked hurt. Or maybe sad, I wasn't sure.

I sat up and closed the book, trying not to slam and yank.

She perched kind of awkwardly on the edge of my bed, and I could tell she wanted to see the journal closer, but I didn't pass it over.

"It looks like it's been through a lot," she finally said.

I gave a little laugh. "You could say that."

She still had that look on her face. Sadness? Hurt? I couldn't tell. But why should she be hurt? Did she think I was saying bad things about her in it? What bad thing could I possibly say?

Then she said, "I used to keep a journal."

"Really?" I asked, and I don't know why, but this seemed very interesting to me. Meg does not seem like the journal-keeping kind.

Of course, then again, neither do I.

"You don't write in it anymore?" I asked.

She shook her head. Then she gave me a knowing look and said, "No one's ever read mine, either."

We both said nothing for a little while. Then very softly she added, "It helped me through a really rough time."

I nodded. "Mine, too."

She looked at my journal again. "You started it when you ran away?"

"A little before."

She reached out and held my hand. "I meant what I said at dinner. You're a real blessing in my life. I hope someday you'll be able to trust me with what you've gone through." Then she gave me a sad smile and said, "It's so hard to talk about, isn't it? Who could possibly

239

understand?" Her eyes were watering as she kissed me on the cheek and said, "I'll see you in the morning."

Now that she's gone to bed, I can't stop wondering:

What in the world happened to *her*?

What "rough time" did her journal help her through?

And what became of it?

Where is that journal now?

Friday afternoon

When I went to use the bathroom this morning, I found a book outside my door.

Meg's journal.

There was a little Post-it on it that said: "Please read. Love, Meg." So I did.

It is absolutely heartbreaking. She was engaged to a man named Randy who was in the air force. His plane was shot down over enemy territory, but his body was never recovered. For years she didn't know if he was dead or alive, a prisoner of war being tortured or just bones decaying in the earth.

The journal covers about six years, then just stops. There's no conclusion, no wrap-up, no happy ending.

It just stops.

When I was done reading it, I darted around the apartment until I found her. She was sitting on the couch in the living room, staring out the window.

"Meg?" I said, and when she looked at me, I threw my arms around her and said, "I'm so sorry!"

She smiled at me, but I could tell she'd been crying.

"Did they ever find him?" I asked.

She shook her head. "That was the hardest part. The not knowing."

"I'm so sorry," I said again.

After a quiet minute she sighed and said, "What I don't think I wrote in there was how much we wanted children. Randy came from a big family and wanted a dozen children."

"A dozen!?"

She laughed, and it was a real laugh. "I told him, 'Four at the most!' and he said, 'Can't we have five?' He thought we had the genetics to produce an outstanding basketball team."

I laughed. "A basketball team?"

She nodded, then took a deep breath and sighed. "I was crazy in love with him."

I put my head on her shoulder. "I could tell."

We were quiet for a long time, and finally she said, "Do you understand why your coming to stay with us has been such a blessing?"

I sat up and looked at her. "I'm not exactly a basketball team. . . ."

Tears sprang to her eyes. "I don't need a basketball team, Holly. Not anymore."

Sunday, November 28th

scraps of love
torn and tattered
faded, scattered
trashed

threads of hope
frayed and tangled
broken, mangled
dashed

backing, buttons
yarn and batting
quilted tenderly
wrapped up in
this warm repair
my patchwork family

Wednesday, December 1st

For days I thought about it, and finally I did it:

I let Meg read this journal.

I understood her so much better after I'd read hers, and since it looks like I am going to be staying here, I want her to understand me, too.

I was really nervous when I gave it to her. My heart was pounding! She asked me, "Are you sure?" so I *could* have snatched it back. But I just winced and said, "Just promise you won't kick me out once you read it, okay?"

She laughed and said, "Of course I won't," but I still worried. The whole time she had it, I worried. I couldn't really remember a lot of what I'd written, but I knew it was brutally honest. Scary honest. Would she think I was an awful person?

And other parts . . . would she think they were stupid? Catty? Crude? Embarrassing?

And the poems . . . oh no, the poems! Were they completely lame?

I kept wondering what was taking her so long.

What was she thinking?

When she finally brought it back to me, she sat beside me on the couch for what felt like an eternity, saying nothing. Her eyes were a little watery, and she didn't seem to want to look at me.

Inside I started to panic. Why had I ever let her read my journal? It said in black and white how great I was at lying and deceiving and stealing . . . why *would* she want me to live with her?

But then she looked at me and whispered, "I am so proud to know you."

It wasn't what I was expecting. "Proud?"

She nodded. "And I am so sorry for all you've been through."

After that we just talked. She asked me a few questions about things in the journal, but she didn't quiz me up about it or anything. We actually talked more about the future. About the good things ahead.

In the middle of all that talking, though, she gave me some advice that, at the time, I thought was crazy. But it's stuck with me, and now I can't seem to get it out of my mind.

She thinks I should send you a copy of this journal, Ms. Leone.

She thinks you'd really want to know.

What happened to me.

What I've been through.

Why it was so hard for me to talk to you.

Everything.

She also thinks I need to thank you for giving me the journal.

For getting me writing.

And . . . she seems to think you'll like my poems.

I don't know about *that*, but I do think she has a point. And what's interesting to me is that I'd forgotten it was you I was talking to in this journal. I'm not sure when the switch happened, but somewhere along the line I stopped venting at you and started writing to . . . some imagined friend? Myself? I don't know, and I guess it doesn't really matter. The important thing is that this journal made me feel less alone. Like I had someone to talk to.

I remember saying (quite a few pages ago) that I felt like I'd solved something inside me, even though I didn't really understand what the puzzle was. Now I see that it was this book, this journal, that helped me feel that way. It helped me sort through a lot of the hurt and anger. Maybe it didn't solve anything, but somehow it gave me strength. It gave me hope. And the truth is, I don't know if I could have survived this journey without it.

While I'm at it, let me confess that there *is* something to the whole poetry thing you pushed on us. I hate to admit it, but I've grown to like it. I think in stanzas sometimes. I play with phrases in my mind. It's not the sissy stuff I used to think it was. It's the raw heart of the matter.

So after mulling it over for a long time, I've decided to take Meg's advice.

I want you to know that I'm okay.

I want you to know that you helped me.

And I want to say thank you.

Thank you for helping me turn the page.

Author's Note

The idea for *Runaway* was sparked by my friend and teaching colleague Greg Sarkisian. When *Sammy Keyes and the Sisters of Mercy* came out in 1999, he read it and, after telling me how great it was (see, what a friend!), he mentioned that he would love to know more about the homeless girl that Sammy rescues in the story.

The instant he said it I knew this book was in my future. The idea just gripped me. How do you become homeless at twelve? How long could you survive on your own? How *did* Holly wind up in a refrigerator box on the banks of a dried-up riverbed? I had the basic story of her life when I wrote *Sisters of Mercy,* but the details? The details would be hard to face. Hard to live with for the year or more it would take me to write it.

When I write a book, I become immersed in the story. I live it. Breathe it. Think about it day and night. People have told me I'm prolific, but what I really am is obsessive. I just can't seem to let things rest. Ever since Greg made that original comment, Holly's been haunting me. She's been there in the back of my mind, waiting for me to face her one on one. Waiting for the time when I would finally tell her story.

I wanted Holly to have her own unique voice, and for her book to have a distinct style. The idea of a journal came to mind, which led me to the thought of journaling as a classroom tool, and then to musing over the myriad ways teachers try to get kids to keep communications open; to let kids know that they're there for them and they *believe* in them.

When plotting a book, I often spend time lying on the couch sort of story-dreaming—I let one cognitive thread lead to the next, then to the next. Sometimes it gets me absolutely nowhere. Sometimes it helps me make connections or devise wickedly wonderful twists of plot. In the case of *Runaway,* it brought me to the idea that Holly's teacher would be the one to give Holly a journal and encourage her to write. And Holly's reaction would, of course, be just as you found it on page one. But still, Holly has no one. Not a soul in the world whom she feels she can trust. So she talks to Ms. Leone through the journal, and long before she's even aware of it, the journal becomes her lifeline, and eventually her most prized possession.

In my own life, I also came to writing from a place of anger. Life seemed devastating and cruel and completely unfair, and I started lashing out about it on paper. Now when I do school visits, I often share my adopted philosophy on dealing with hard times: Don't take your anger out on yourself (through drugs or alcohol or whatever), don't take it out on other people (by being negative or aggressive or just plain mean), take it out on paper. Getting your anger or sadness or frustration out of your system and onto paper is very cheap and very real therapy. Of course that's a simplistic view of dealing with anger, but in my case, writing saved me from the despair I was feeling, and over time it has evolved into an amazing, joyful career. So I'm a believer, man. A big believer in the power of words!

Anyway, for over a year I've been living in Holly's world, learning about everything from horse trailers to the Los Angeles River, interviewing people, sneaking inside the cargo hold of a Greyhound bus, and yes, spending time at homeless shelters. A lot of this research was sobering, but not unfamiliar. My husband and I lived the first years of our marriage in a run-down four-hundred-square-foot rental house in a bad part of town. Gang activity, domestic violence, drug deals, and homelessness were all present in our neighborhood. We got two big dogs and shut the blinds, but we were never blind to what was going on around us. This was the environment that spawned the character of Holly in the first place.

Ridiculous as it sounds, it was facing poetry that actually scared me the most. I'm an embarrassingly emotional person, and getting down to the "raw heart of the matter" was terrifying to me. I was not a poet—how could I write poems? Even through the voice of Holly, what made me think I could pull this off?

But I had this *ideaaaa,* and anyone who knows me, knows that when I have an *ideaaaa,* there's trouble brewin'. I'm like a dog with a bone. I chew on it and chew on it and just won't let it go. So I chewed on poetry. I studied it, I practiced it, and eventually I got almost comfortable with it. And I'm glad I faced my fears. The poems express Holly's emotions in a way that her narration alone couldn't. There are no walls in her poems, no posturing; just Holly as she really is: vulnerable, scared, and alone.

As always when creating a book, there were people who gave invaluable insight, information, and support. Top of the list is my intelligent, compassionate, versatile, and astute editor, Nancy Siscoe. (Hey, gushing's allowed—this woman pulled me out of the slush pile.) Right beside her is my rock of a husband, fellow writer, and partner in everything, Mark Parsons. Then there's Ginger Knowlton at Curtis Brown, Ltd., who's a lot more than an agent, and my new and very sharp manuscript readers, Colton and Connor. On the research end of things, there's Steve Rodarte at the San Luis Obispo Greyhound Station, plus the actual driver who busted me but didn't have me arrested (and instead showed me how you could escape the cargo hold), Nancy Herzog-Johnson, a friend and longtime volunteer at the Prado Lane homeless shelter, and Whitney, the girl at the shelter who told me her story while I was "under cover."

Those people have my sincere thanks, but the *dedication* of this book goes to a group that doesn't hear thank you enough—teachers. Teachers like Ms. Leone. The ones who are determined to reach the kid who seems unreachable. The ones who put their heart and soul into their profession and often don't know the outcome of their efforts. The ones who care enough to make a difference, even if they're never thanked.

This book I dedicate to them.

Here's a sneak peek at another powerful novel from Wendelin Van Draanen

FROM THE AUTHOR OF *FLIPPED*

Wendelin Van Draanen

The Running Dream

AVAILABLE NOW!

Excerpt copyright © 2011 by Wendelin Van Draanen Parsons. Published in the
United States by Alfred A. Knopf, an imprint of Random House Children's Books,
a division of Penguin Random House LLC, New York.

chapter 1

MY LIFE IS OVER.

Behind the morphine dreams is the nightmare of reality.

A reality I can't face.

I cry myself back to sleep, wishing, pleading, praying that I'll wake up from this, but the same nightmare always awaits me.

"Shhh," my mother whispers. "It'll be okay." But her eyes are swollen and red, and I know she doesn't believe what she's saying.

My father—now that's a different story. He doesn't even try to lie to me. What's the use? He knows what this means.

My hopes, my dreams, my life . . . it's over.

The only one who seems unfazed is Dr. Wells. "Hello there, Jessica!" he says. I don't know if it's day or night. The second day or the first. "How are you feeling?"

I just stare at him. What am I supposed to say, Fine?

He inspects my chart. "So let's have a look, shall we?"

He pulls the covers off my lap, and I find myself face to face with the truth.

My right leg has no foot.

No ankle.

No shin.

It's just my thigh, my knee, and a stump wrapped in a mountain of gauze.

My eyes flood with tears as Dr. Wells removes the bandages and inspects his handiwork. I turn away, only to see my mother fighting back tears of her own. "It'll be okay," she tells me, holding tight to my hand. "We'll get through this."

Dr. Wells is maddeningly cheerful. "This looks excellent, Jessica. Nice vascular flow, good color . . . you're already healing beautifully."

I glance at the monstrosity below my knee.

It's red and bulging at the end. Fat staples run around my stump like a big ugly zipper, and the skin is stained dirty yellow.

"How's the pain?" he asks. "Are you managing okay?"

I wipe away my tears and nod, because the pain in my leg is nothing compared to the one in my heart.

None of their meds will make that one go away.

He goes on, cheerfully. "I'll order a shrinker sock to control the swelling. Your residual limb will be very tender for a while, and applying the shrinker sock may be uncomfortable at first, but it's important to get you into one. Reducing the swelling and shaping your limb is the first step in your rehabilitation." A nurse appears to re-bandage me as he makes notes in my chart and says, "A prosthetist will be in later today to apply it."

Tears continue to run down my face.

I don't seem to have the strength to hold them back.

Dr. Wells softens. "The surgery went beautifully, Jessica." He says this like he's trying to soothe away reality. "And considering everything, you're actually very lucky. You're alive, and you still have your knee, which makes a huge difference in your future mobility. BK amputees have it much easier than AK amputees."

"BK? AK?" my mom asks.

"I'm sorry," he says, turning to my mother. "Below knee. Above knee. In the world of prosthetic legs, it's a critical difference." He prepares to leave. "There will obviously be an adjustment period, but Jessica is young and fit, and I have full confidence that she will return to a completely normal life."

My mother nods, but she seems dazed. Like she's wishing my father was there to help her absorb what's being said.

Dr. Wells flashes a final smile at me. "Focus on the positive, Jessica. We'll have you up and walking again in short order."

This from the man who sawed off my leg.

He whooshes from the room, leaving a dark, heavy cloud of the unspoken behind.

My mother smiles and coos reassuringly, but she knows what I'm thinking.

What does it matter?

I'll never run again.

chapter 2

I AM A RUNNER.

    That's what I do.

    That's who I am.

    Running is all I know, or want, or care about.

    It was a race around the soccer field in third grade that swept me into a real love of running.

    Breathing the sweet smell of spring grass.

    Sailing over dots of blooming clover.

    Beating all the boys.

    After that, I couldn't stop. I ran everywhere. Raced everyone. I loved the wind across my cheeks, through my hair.

    Running aired out my soul.

    It made me feel *alive*.

    And now?

    I'm stuck in this bed, knowing I'll never run again.

chapter 3

THE PROSTHETIST IS STOCKY and bald, and he tells me to call him Hank. He tries to talk to me about a fake leg, but I make him stop.

I just can't listen to this.

He gets the nurse to put a new bandage on my leg. One that's thinner. With less gauze.

I'm cold.

The room's cold.

Everything feels cold.

I want to cover up, but Hank is getting ready to put on the shrinker sock. It's like a long, toeless tube sock. He pulls it through a short length of wide PVC pipe, then folds the top part of the sock back over the pipe. I don't understand what he's going to do with it, and I don't care.

Until he slips the pipe over my stump.

"Oh!" I gasp as pressure and pain shoot up my leg.

"I'm sorry," Hank says, transferring the sock from the pipe onto my leg as he pulls the pipe off. "We're almost done."

Half the tube sock is now dangling from my stump. Hank slides a small ring up the dangling end, then stretches out the rest of the sock and doubles it up over the ring and over my stump.

There's pressure. Throbbing. But Hank assures me it'll feel better soon. "The area is swollen," he tells me. "Pooling with blood. The shrinker sock will help reduce the swelling and speed your recovery. Once the wound is healed and the volume of your leg is reduced, we can fit you with a preparatory prosthesis."

"How long will that take?" my mother asks. Her voice starts out shaky, but she tries to steady it.

Hank whips out a soft tape measure and circles the end of my stump. "That's hard to say."

His mind seems to wander, so my mom asks, "Well, in a typical situation?"

Hank takes a deep breath. "Typical is a person in poor health. Someone with circulatory problems. Someone who's old, overweight, or suffering from diabetes." He glances at me. "A case like Jessica's will not have the same timeline. Her recovery will be much quicker."

"So what is *their* expected recovery time?" my mother asks, and she's sounding testy.

"We usually don't fit them with a preparatory prosthesis for about six months."

"Six months?" my mother gasps.

"But Jessica could have hers in a fraction of that time. It all depends on her healing and how soon she can tolerate it."

They talk some more, but I stop listening.

What does it matter how long it takes?

I'll never recover.

I can't see how I'll ever even adjust.

chapter 4

I CLOSE MY EYES and drift off.

I see the race.

Vanessa Steele's in lane five, stretching out. Her long nails painted deep red, her racing glasses flashing back the late-morning sun.

I remember thinking that Vanessa has been good for me. Her superior attitude, her mind games, her domination of the 400-meter.

It's been good for me.

Vanessa glances over her shoulder, waiting for me to get into my blocks before she gets down in hers.

It's part of her game. She likes to be the last one standing.

This time I don't mind. I'm through being sucked into her psych-out.

I feel calm.

Confident.

Kyro has been helping me focus. He's been building me up mentally and physically, coaching me for this moment.

I give Vanessa a little smile and nod from my position in lane four. She's in red and yellow—Langston High's colors.

I'm in Liberty High's blue and gold. Even my colors feel light—like the sun and the sky floating above me.

I'm down in the blocks now, ready to fly.

Vanessa makes her final adjustments, then holds steady.

The gun goes off and all runners shoot forward. It's a fury of steps, spikes against track. They thunder all around me but somehow sound miles away.

By the first bend we find our stride. My kick is good. Strong and long.

Whoosh, whoosh, whoosh, whoosh!

My arms are pumping, but they're smooth, almost relaxed.

Whoosh, whoosh, whoosh, whoosh!

My breathing's open, flowing, and I barely feel my feet touching down.

Whoosh, whoosh, whoosh, whoosh!

Suddenly I'm floating.

Flying.

Soaring around the track.

The thunder fades behind me, and the staggered start has me at a mental advantage—I can see Vanessa, but she can only feel me behind her, moving in.

At the 200-meter mark the field has widened.

All except for Vanessa and me.

We've tightened.

We crest at the 300, then face Rigor Mortis Bend.

Vanessa knows I'm here.

On her tail.

We're down to grit and guts, so I dig in.

Dig deep.

She does the same.

We battle along the straightaway, my legs burning, aching, empty. Shoulder to shoulder, I force one last push and duck over the finish line in front of her.

"Fifty-five flat!" Kyro shouts. "Fifty-five flat!"

It's a new personal best for me.

A new record for the league.

It's also the last race of my life.

My finish line.

chapter 5

NURSES COME IN AND OUT. Conversations happen around me. Whispers, like a heavy fog, hang on in my mind.

But then there's my father's voice.

And Dr. Wells's.

Outside my room their words drift in through the crack in the doorway.

My father asks about things he's researched online. Rigid removable dressings. Speedier recoveries. I-pops. He sounds like a doctor.

Dr. Wells's replies revolve around small-town practicalities, insurance allowances, and the tried-and-true methods employed by Mercy Hospital.

Dad comes in and checks on me, and although he pretends to be upbeat, he's irked. He likes to fix things. Now.

He checks out the stump protector that's been put on over the shrinker sock. It holds my leg straight and keeps me from bumping the wound. He seems pleased with it and throws around phrases like "controlling edema" and "preventing knee flexion contracture."

He sounds like he knows what he's talking about.
But really he's a self-employed handyman.
And I'm not something he can fix.

Don't miss these other terrific novels from Wendelin Van Draanen

Wendelin Van Draanen

FLIPPED

New bonus material inside!

FROM THE AUTHOR OF *FLIPPED*

Wendelin Van Draanen

The Running Dream

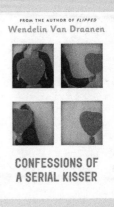

FROM THE AUTHOR OF *FLIPPED*

Wendelin Van Draanen

CONFESSIONS OF A SERIAL KISSER

"We flipped over this fantastic book, its gutsy girl Juli and its wise, wonderful ending."
—*Chicago Tribune*

"Jessica's determination and passion will touch everyone who reads this story."
—*The Examiner*

"The playful title and premise are matched by tender and convincing storytelling."
—*Publishers Weekly*